Leap, Frog

JANE CUTLER

Leap, Frog

Pictures by
TRACEY CAMPBELL PEARSON

Farrar Straus Giroux   New York

Text copyright © 2002 by Jane Cutler
Pictures copyright © 2002 by Tracey Campbell Pearson
All rights reserved
Distributed in Canada by Douglas & McIntyre Ltd.
Printed in the United States of America
Designed by Nancy Goldenberg
First edition, 2002
1 3 5 7 9 10 8 6 4 2

Library of Congress Cataloging-in-Publication Data
Cutler, Jane.
    Leap, frog / Jane Cutler ; pictures by Tracey Campbell Pearson.
        p.   cm.
    Summary: Edward and his new friend Charley prepare for the First
Annual Mark Twain Memorial Jumping Frog Contest.
    ISBN 0-374-34362-4
    [1. Frogs–Fiction.   2. Contests–Fiction.]   I. Pearson, Tracey Campbell,
ill.   II. Title.

PZ7.C985 Le 2002
[Fic]–dc21

                                                                        2001054456

For my editor, Margaret Ferguson
—JC

For Max . . . ribbit . . . ribbit
—TCP

Contents

Leap, Frog

The New Kid

On Saturday morning, Jason and Edward Fraser sat on their front steps. They were watching two moving men load Mr. and Mrs. Miller's furniture into a gigantic moving van, while the Millers' grownup son, Jack, supervised. Their friends Elaine Abrams and Marilyn and Marlene Conroy were sitting on the steps watching, too.

They had all said goodbye to Mr. and Mrs. Miller at the neighborhood potluck dinner held in the Millers' honor before they left. But now, seeing the furniture carried out of the Millers' house and loaded into a moving van made them understand that their neighbors really were gone.

"When I was little, Mrs. Miller taught me how to tie my shoes," said Elaine sadly.

"She taught me how to tell time," said Jason.

"She taught me how to tie my shoes, and how to tell time, and how to make play dough out of flour and water and salt," said Marilyn.

"She taught me how to tie my shoes and tell time and make play dough and bake sugar cookies," said her sister Marlene.

"She taught me how to tie my shoes and tell time and make play dough and bake sugar cookies and plant seeds," announced Marilyn, standing up.

"She taught me how to tie my shoes and tell time and make play dough and bake cookies and plant seeds and play 'Chopsticks' on the piano!" declared Marlene, standing up, too.

Jason and Elaine looked worried. But Edward didn't seem to notice that the Conroy twins, who always agreed with each other, were having a fight.

"She taught me how to tie my shoes and tell time and make play dough and bake cookies and plant seeds and play 'Chopsticks' and fly a kite!" shouted Marilyn.

The girls folded their arms over their chests and glared at each other.

"Me too," said Edward, sighing.

"You too what?" demanded Marilyn.

"Yeah, what?" demanded Marlene.

"I'm going to miss Mrs. Miller, too," he replied.

The friends were silent. The twins sat back down, and everyone watched until the last piece of the Millers' furniture was carried out of the house and Jack and the moving van drove away.

They were just getting up when another, even bigger moving van came and parked in front of the empty house. Two burly men jumped out of the cab, opened the back of the van, and started to unload boxes and furniture. Then a car drove up and parked.

"The new family," observed Marilyn, sitting down again.

"Mmmm," agreed Marlene, sitting down beside her sister.

Elaine and Jason and Edward sat down again, too.

The new family got out of their car. One man. One woman. And one first-grade-sized child, wearing a white karate outfit with a yellow belt and high-topped white athletic shoes that winked and blinked red and green and purple lights every time he took a step.

When the new boy saw the kids sitting on the

steps, he put his hands on his hips and stared at them. Then he yelled, "Hi-*ya!*" and executed some karate kicks and chops in their direction.

"Hi," called Marilyn. The boy stared at her.

"What's your name?" called Marlene.

"Hi-*ya!*" the boy cried again, chopping and kicking. Then he stood still and stared at all of them.

"I'm Edward," Edward said loudly. "This is my brother, Jason. This is Elaine. This is Marilyn. And this is Marlene." He stopped to think. "Or maybe it's the other way around. I can't always tell."

Now the Conroy twins both glared at Edward. "You *can't?*" they said.

"I never knew that!" said Marlene. She was put out.

"Neither did I," said Marilyn. *She* was put out.

"What about you, Jason?" said Marlene. "Can you tell us apart?"

"Of course I can," said Jason.

"Who am I, then?" asked Marlene.

"You're Marlene," Elaine said.

"I was asking *Jason*," said the twin.

"We can all tell you apart," Jason interrupted. "At least, most of the time we can."

"I always can," said Edward.

Now everyone stared at him again. "You just said you couldn't," said Marilyn.

"Just a minute ago!" said Marlene.

"I didn't mean it," said Edward.

"Then why did you say it?" threatened Marlene.

"Yeah, why?" echoed her sister.

"Let me think," said Edward, pressing his fist against his forehead and frowning so the twins could see how hard he was thinking.

"Hey!" called the new boy. "What about *me*?"

"What about you?" said Marlene and Marilyn.

"I'm new," he answered.

"And you're . . ." prompted Jason, still trying to find out the new kid's name.

"And I'm *wild*!" the boy cried. He ran around in circles to show them just how wild he was.

"What I meant was, what's your name?" Jason told him.

"Halliburton Charles Pembroke O'Hara," the boy cried, marking each word with a karate chop or a kick.

"Some name!" exclaimed Marilyn. "What do people call you?"

"Yeah!" echoed Marlene. "What do people call you?"

The boy stood still. "What does who call me?" he wanted to know.

"Your parents," said Elaine.

"Your teachers," said Jason.

"Your friends," said Edward.

The boy frowned. "I'm new," he said finally. "I don't have any friends. Hi-*ya*!" He started kicking and chopping all over again.

Just then his mother came back outside. She smiled in a pleasant way at the kids sitting on the steps. Then she walked across the lawn and put her hand on top of her son's head.

"Charley," she said, "lift your shoulders." He lifted his shoulders. "Touch your knee." He touched his knee. "Pinch your nose." He giggled and pinched his nose. "Come with me."

Charley and his mother went into the Millers' house, which was their house now.

"Some kid," said Jason, annoyed.

"Yeah, what a great new neighbor," said Elaine, disappointed.

The friends watched the moving men work a while longer. Soon Marlene and Marilyn got bored. They hopped on their scooters and headed home. Then Andrew Kelly turned up, and he and Jason and Elaine went inside.

But Edward stayed. He pulled a smashed apricot oat bar out of his jeans pocket, opened it up, and munched on it while he thought about the Millers' furniture being carried out and the new people's furniture being carried in. Seeing the furniture leave had made him feel sad. But watching the furniture come had made him feel better.

Pretty soon Charley came out and stood by his own front door. He had a carton of milk with a straw in it and a paper plate with a sandwich on it. He looked over at the steps. When he saw Edward sitting there, he walked across the lawn that separated the two houses and sat down, putting the milk and the plate on the step between them.

Edward munched his apricot oat bar and eyed the fresh-looking peanut butter and jelly sandwich. Charley picked up half of the sandwich and took a bite. Beautiful purple jelly dribbled onto his chin.

After he chewed and swallowed and noisily sucked up some milk, Charley said, "What do you get if you cross a helicopter with a skunk?"

Edward pretended he'd never heard the joke before. "Mmmm," he said. Charley smiled.

Edward frowned, to show he was trying hard to think of the answer.

Charley started to giggle and put his hands

over his mouth, to keep from blurting out the punch line.

"I don't know," Edward fibbed. "What?"

"A *smellicopter*!" cried Charley.

Edward fake-laughed and slapped his knee. "That's a good one," he said.

"Yeah," said Charley, very pleased. He handed the other half of his sandwich to Edward, and Edward gave him what was left of the apricot oat bar. They ate and watched the movers carry in the rest of the family's things.

"You have to go now," Edward said after a while.

"I do?" said Charley.

"Yep. You have to go home."

"Why?"

" 'Cause I've got stuff to do."

"Me too," said Charley, jumping up. "I've got a lot of stuff to do." He left his empty milk carton, his straw, and his paper plate on the steps and took off.

"See ya!" called Edward.

"Hi-*ya*!" shouted Charley.

"See ya *later*," Edward called.

"Alligator," yelled Charley.

"Soon, I *hope*," Edward called back.

"Antelope!" hollered Charley.

11

"After a *while*," sang out Edward.

"Crocodile!" screamed Charley. "Hi-*ya*!"

Charley took off his yellow belt and swung it over his head like a lasso as he tore across the lawn. The red, green, and purple lights in his shoes winked wildly as he ran.

Egg Babies

Edward picked up the trash Charley had left. He didn't have his key, and he felt too lazy to go around back, so he rang the front doorbell. He waited. Nobody came. He rang again and waited. Nobody came. He rang three times. "Hold your horses, I'm coming," called Mrs. Fraser.

Edward wondered why his mother, who was usually quick, was taking so long.

Finally, she opened the door. "Sorry," she said. "I can't walk very well yet in these new shoes."

Edward looked at her feet. She had on black shoes with huge soles and no fronts or backs. And she seemed to be having trouble standing up in them.

13

Edward didn't want to hurt his mother's feelings. He knew she always liked to have the very latest style of shoes, if she could.

"Maybe you got the wrong size?" he said.

Mrs. Fraser looked at her feet. "No," she said, "these are the size they're supposed to be."

"Really?" Edward asked.

"Really."

"Are you sure? Did you ask the salesman to check and see where your toes are?"

"It doesn't matter where my toes are, Edward," said Mrs. Fraser, shuffling off. "These shoes don't have any fronts. I'm sure I'll get the hang of walking in them soon. Rome wasn't built in a day, you know."

"Rome?"

"Ancient Rome."

"Ancient Rome?"

"Oh yes, he's home," his mother said, concentrating on her clumsy retreat.

"Who?"

"Jason," Mrs. Fraser replied over her shoulder. "Didn't you say 'Is Jason home?' "

"No, I said—never mind—yes, that's what I said. Is Jason home?"

"Yep," his mother replied. "He and Andrew and Elaine are in the family room."

The family room door was open. Jason and Elaine and Andrew were sitting on the floor in front of the couch, talking.

"Knock-knock!" said Edward brightly.

The three older kids looked up. Jason said, "Who's. There." What he meant was, "This better be good."

"Just me, Jason," said Edward, giggling. "Who'd you think it was?" He plopped down on the floor with the others. "So what are we talking about?" he asked.

"*We* are talking about stuff that has nothing to do with you," Jason replied.

Edward made a face at his brother.

"Well, we're talking about stuff that has nothing to do with you, too," Elaine reminded Jason.

"It has more to do with me than it does with him," Jason protested.

"How do you figure?" Andrew wanted to know.

"Well, I'm in middle school with you guys now and I'll be in Mr. Z.'s class next year, when I'm in seventh grade, and Edward won't be in it for three years after that. And by then Mr. Z. might have changed his curriculum, or gone to teach at another school."

"The fact is," Elaine replied, "Andrew and I are in seventh grade and in Mr. Z.'s class right now.

We're the ones with the problem. You and Edward aren't involved."

"Then why are you here?" Edward wanted to know.

"Yeah, why?" asked Jason, switching sides.

"Because you're our friends," said Elaine.

"You're both our friends," said Andrew.

"And to whom can you turn in times of trouble, if not to your friends?" said Elaine, quoting something she'd heard her mother say.

"Times of trouble," Edward repeated. He liked the sound of it. Then he thought about the meaning. "What's the trouble?" he asked eagerly.

"It's Mr. Z.'s Sex-Ed class," Andrew explained.

"Sex-Ed class?" asked Edward. "What's that?"

"It's a new class," said Elaine.

"It's required," said Andrew.

"But what is it?" Edward persisted.

"New," mumbled Andrew, looking at the floor.

"Required," sang Elaine, looking at the ceiling.

"About *sex*," said Jason, looking at Edward.

"Sex!" exclaimed Edward happily. "In school!"

"See?" Jason said to Elaine and Andrew. "What did I tell you?"

"This is not getting us anyplace," said sensible Elaine. "Here's what's happening, Edward. Right now, in Mr. Z.'s new, required Sex-Ed class, we're studying about babies."

"Babies!" said Edward. "Cool!"

"About taking care of them," offered Andrew. "About what it's like being a full-time parent and having to take care of a little baby. The unit is called Parenting: Are You Ready?"

"Where are you getting the babies?" Edward asked excitedly, getting up on his knees.

"From the SPCA," cracked Jason.

"Baby animals?" asked Edward.

"Jason, quit it," said Andrew.

"Okay, okay," said Jason.

"That's what we have to decide Monday in class," Elaine said. "We have to vote on what kind of babies we want to have."

"We have a choice," Andrew continued. "We can have egg babies, or we can have five-pound-sack-of-flour babies."

"We have to vote. Majority wins," Elaine added.

"So if eggs get the most votes, we have to carry an egg around with us every single place we go, day and night, for a whole week," Andrew explained. "And if sacks of flour get the most votes, we have to carry a sack of flour with us everywhere we go for a whole week."

"And Andrew and I are trying to decide how to vote," concluded Elaine.

"And I'm trying to help them decide," said Jason, giving Edward a look.

"And I'm trying to help them decide, too," countered Edward, giving Jason a look back and sitting down again.

"I'm for sacks of flour," said Elaine. "Because that would be more like carrying a real baby."

"And I'm for eggs," said Andrew, "because a sack of flour could feel awfully heavy after a while."

"Wait a minute," said Edward. "Eggs would break. Splat! There goes the baby!"

"If we do eggs, we can drain the inside stuff out of them. Then we have just the shell," Elaine explained. "It would be really delicate. But it wouldn't splat."

"Or we can hard-boil them," Andrew reminded her.

"Hard-boiled babies!" cried Edward. Jason started to giggle. So did Edward. Elaine and Andrew didn't laugh.

"Let's go, Andrew," said Elaine, standing up. "I don't think Jason and Edward are going to be able to help us with this."

"Guess not," said Andrew, standing up, too.

"Hey, wait," cried Jason, scrambling to his feet and wiping the grin off his face. "I'll help! I promise!"

Off he went after Elaine and Andrew.

Edward didn't follow them. He lay on his back with his hands under his head and looked at the family room ceiling. It was painted white, and the paint had gold and silver sparkles in it. His father thought the sparkles were tacky. But his mother loved them. She had even mixed extra sparkles into the paint when she repainted the ceiling.

Edward loved the sparkles, too. Now, as he let his eyes travel over the very agreeable sparkly ceiling, he thought about babies. Or rather, he thought about eggs. Egg babies. You could draw faces on them with Magic Markers, he thought. You could make hats for them out of scraps of cloth or out of construction paper. You could make a bed for an egg baby in a tiny basket or in a cardboard box lined with cotton. You could name your egg baby and write its name on the side of the box. Or if you had a basket, you could decorate it with all different colored ribbons and strings. You could paste yarn hair on your egg baby, or you could leave it bald.

The more Edward thought about all the things you could do with an egg baby, the more he wanted one. Soon he wanted an egg baby more than anything. He felt he had to have one right that minute.

Edward jumped to his feet and raced to the kitchen. He opened the refrigerator door and peered inside. Ah! A carton of eggs. He took it out and set it on the counter. Happy Hens Eggs, it said.

Just the thing for an egg baby, Edward thought. A happy egg from a happy hen! How many eggs were left? He opened the carton. Twelve eggs. Edward looked down at them. Which one did he want to be his baby?

It was impossible to tell, just looking from the top. All he could see was the colors, from dark brown to almost white.

He took a towel out of the drawer and spread it on the counter. Then, carefully, he took each egg out of the carton and set it gently on the towel.

When the eggs were all out of the carton, Edward lifted up each one and examined it. He took off his glasses so he could take advantage of being nearsighted and see every single thing about each egg. To his surprise, eggs—which he had always thought of as looking pretty much alike—turned out to be unique. This one was much more pointy than the rest, and that one much more rounded.

Here was one with a rough place on one part of its shell. Two had freckles, but one of these had small freckles and one had big ones. Another egg had lines that looked like scratches. And here was one with a shell that was crinkled at one end. Some of the eggs were uneven, with little bulges here and there. Some were perfectly even, just like the eggs in drawings and photographs.

The more Edward studied each egg, the more special it seemed, and the more he liked it. The better he got to know each one, the more he wanted that one to be his egg baby. Finally, he got to know all twelve of the eggs so well there was no way he could choose one over the others.

He would just have to have a dozen egg babies!

As Edward stood looking affectionately at all the eggs, his mother came into the kitchen. She was walking easily, wearing tennis shoes, spanking new white ones. "Making an omelette, Edward?" she asked.

Edward frowned at her and shook his head no.

"Egg salad?"

"No."

"Egg*plant*?" she joked.

"Nope. Egg babies."

"Eggbabies? What's that? A new recipe? Can we have it for dinner?"

21

"Have what for dinner?" asked Edward.

"What you're making," his mother replied. "Eggbabies."

"Dinner!" exclaimed Edward. "No way! Do you think I'd let you eat my babies?"

"Your babies?" Mrs. Fraser asked. Edward nodded yes.

"Your *egg* babies?" she inquired. Edward nodded again.

Mrs. Fraser pushed her rhinestone-studded cat's-eye glasses up on top of her head and closed her eyes so she could think clearly. "May I ask you a question, Edward?" she said finally.

"What about?"

"Eggs."

"Eggs. Sure." Edward carefully put all the eggs back into the carton.

His mother reached over, picked up the carton of eggs, and held it in her hands. "About these eggs," she repeated.

"Oh, *these* eggs!" cried Edward, now giving her his attention. "What about them?"

"Just what I was going to ask *you*," replied his mother. "What about them?"

"Well," Edward explained, "I was hoping you'd sell me these eggs. And show me how to get rid of the insides without breaking the shells."

"Yes?" prompted his mother.

"And then I was going to draw faces on them and make hats for them and beds for them and give them names and take them with me wherever I go. Just like real babies."

Mrs. Fraser put the carton of eggs back down on the counter. "For heaven's sake, *why*?" she asked.

"That's what Elaine and Andrew have to do. And everybody else in Mr. Z.'s seventh-grade Sex-Ed class."

"You're not in Mr. Z.'s Sex-Ed class, Edward," his mother reminded him. "Right now you're a third-grader."

"I know that, Mom," Edward said reasonably.

Mrs. Fraser paused. Then she started over. "What I mean is, why do you think Mr. Z. is having the kids in his class carry around fragile egg babies with them wherever they go?"

"Or five-pound bags of flour," Edward remembered. "The class gets to vote. But I think eggs are better."

"Whichever one," his mother replied. "It's still the same idea. Why do you think Mr. Z. wants the kids in Sex-Ed to carry a pretend baby with them every single place they go?"

Edward knew the answer to that one. He

24

grinned at his mother. "So they can see how much fun it is to have babies!" he replied.

"Well, partly that," Mrs. Fraser hedged. "But also . . ."

"So they can see what it'll be like to be moms and dads when they grow up!" Edward answered happily.

"Well, yes," his mother said again, slowly. "Partly that, too. But also so . . ."

"So?" asked Edward.

"So . . . well, I hate to be the one to break it to you, Edward," said Mrs. Fraser, "but also so they can see how hard it is to take care of a baby all the time. I think Mr. Z. wants his students to understand that having babies isn't fun and games. He wants them to understand that you really have to be—mature—before you even *think* about having a baby."

Edward frowned. "I don't think so, Mom," he said. "See, they're talking about eggs or sacks of flour. It's all pretend. I think Mr. Z. wants his class to have fun playing house with pretend babies.

"Nobody in Mr. Z.'s class is old enough to have a real baby. So he wouldn't bother with all that serious stuff and waste their time in school. Teachers are strict about wasting time, you know.

"Maybe it was different when you were in school, Mom," he concluded kindly. "Anyway, how much for the eggs?"

Mrs. Fraser gave up. "Are you planning to use all twelve?" she asked.

Edward nodded. "Twelve."

"A lot of babies."

"Yep," Edward agreed. "So how much do a dozen eggs cost, Mom? Will you sell these to me?"

"Oh, you can just have them, Edward. I'll get some more next time I go to the market."

"Thanks, Mom."

"But don't forget to keep them in the fridge until you get the insides out of them," she warned, "or they could start to rot."

"Rotten babies." Edward chuckled.

"You know," continued his mother, "you could hard-boil them."

"Boiled babies." Edward chuckled.

"They'll last for at least a week, boiled, and they'll be much less fragile."

"I'm going to want them for more than a week," Edward said.

"If you want them for longer than they last, you can always boil up another batch," said Mrs. Fraser. "It'd be better than having broken babies."

"I have to think about it," he decided. "But just in case I want to empty them out, can you tell me how to do it?"

His mother thought. "Well, you take something small and sharp—like a mini-screwdriver or a skinny skewer—and you stick it in one end of the egg and push it out the other. And then you let the insides drain out.

"You have to make sure you run the sharp thing through the yolk and that all the yolk drains. If it doesn't, what's left will spoil and smell awful.

"Once the insides are out, all you've got is the really fragile shell. It'll be a challenge to take care of that, I can tell you." She thought for a moment. "It'll feel sort of like taking care of a tiny, brand-new human baby. You'll be scared to death."

This thought seemed to make Mrs. Fraser feel rather cheerful, and she began to rummage through the kitchen junk drawer, looking for a skewer.

Finally, she held one out to Edward. "Here you go," she said. "Take one of those eggs, and just shove this right down through it, top to bottom. Do it over the sink so the inside stuff can run down the drain. Here."

Mrs. Fraser had to put the skewer into Edward's hand. Then she had to give him an egg.

Then she had to take him by the shoulders and steer him over to the sink. "Edward," she said, "what's the problem?"

"No problem, Mom," Edward said quietly.

"Well then, stab away!" advised his mother.

With his left hand, Edward took a firm hold on the skewer. With his right hand, he took a firm hold on the egg. He took such a firm hold on the egg he crushed it. His left hand held the skewer ready. But his right hand was full of broken bits of eggshell and a lot of slimy stuff.

"Yuck!" he exclaimed.

"If at first you don't succeed . . ." his mother reminded him.

Edward put down the skewer and washed and dried his hand. He picked up the skewer again. His mother handed him another egg.

This time, Edward took a firm hold on the skewer, but he held the egg much more gently. He readied the skewer. He eyed the egg. He saw it was one of the freckled ones. A pointy-headed freckled one, with a friendly look.

Edward put the sharp skewer right up against its pointy head and, very gently, pushed. Nothing happened. He pushed a little harder. Still nothing happened. He was going to push harder—but he couldn't. He could not bring himself to impale this friendly-looking freckled egg on a sharp skewer. He put down the skewer and turned to his mother, who stood waiting.

"You know," he said, "Andrew said it was better to boil them. I think that *would* be better. That way they won't be so fragile and hard to take care of. I mean, I am going to have to take care of twelve—eleven—of them. I think I'll boil them instead. How do you do that?"

"That *is* a whole lot easier," his mother agreed. "Just take a pot big enough to hold them all. Fill it almost full of water. Pour in some salt to keep the shells from cracking. Turn on the heat, and bring the water to a boil. Then put each egg onto this slotted spoon—you've seen me do this before, Edward—and lower it into the water. Let the eggs boil for about ten minutes. Then turn off the heat, and leave the eggs in the water until they cool down. Couldn't be easier," said Mrs. Fraser. She handed Edward the slotted spoon and left the kitchen.

Edward put salt and water into a large pot and waited until the water came to a boil. Then he chose an egg and set it carefully on the slotted spoon. As he started to lower it into the bubbling water, he remembered how it felt when the water in the bathtub was too hot and he started to get in. He knew the water in the tub was nowhere near as hot as this boiling water was.

For a moment, Edward stood holding the egg over the pot of water. Then, carefully, he put it down and turned off the heat.

He had to face it: he wasn't ready. He couldn't skewer his babies, and he couldn't boil them. He wasn't mature enough to have babies. He would have to wait until he was older, when he'd be able to do these things without feeling bad. Then he would be ready to have an egg baby. Now he was still too much of a baby himself.

Monday evening Jason got an e-mail from Elaine. It said, "The class voted for eggs. We had a grab bag. I got twin girls. I'm boiling."

He got an e-mail from Andrew. It said, "We're doing eggs. I got a girl. Elaine got twins. The whole class is boiling."

Edward also got an e-mail from Elaine. It said, "I'm the mother of twin girls. They're boiled. They're identical. But they're just eggs. I don't care anything about them. Maybe if you drew faces on them it would help."

Edward loved to draw. He couldn't wait to draw faces on Elaine's identical twin egg babies. He had brand-new Magic Markers with extra-thin points that would be perfect for drawing faces on eggshells. When he got through with those eggs, Elaine would care about them.

Edward e-mailed back, "Sure. Come over after school tomorrow."

Then Edward got an e-mail from Andrew. It said, "My little sister scribbled on one side of my egg. Could you help me paste some hair or something over that side and make a face on the other side? I might like it better if it wasn't so messed up."

Edward wrote back, "Come over after school tomorrow."

"Okay," replied Andrew.

Edward was halfway in and halfway out of his closet, rummaging in the big paper sacks where he kept his art supplies, when Jason came into his room.

"They decided to do eggs," Jason said.

"I know," Edward replied. His voice coming from inside the closet was hard to hear.

"What?" said Jason.

"I know," Edward shouted.

"What?" Jason shouted back.

Edward backed out of his closet. "I know!" he screamed.

"You don't have to holler," Jason scolded. "How do you know?"

"Elaine and Andrew e-mailed me," said Edward, "that's how."

"E-mailed *you*," replied Jason, annoyed.

"E-mailed *me*," replied Edward.

"Why would they e-mail you?" Jason asked.

"Why wouldn't they e-mail me?" Edward answered.

Jason was stumped. "Well, why would they?" he repeated.

"They e-mailed me because they want me to draw faces on their egg babies," said Edward, "that's why."

"Oh, well then," said Jason, walking out of Edward's room.

Edward shook his head. He would never understand his brother. Never. Why waste time trying? He pulled the bags of art supplies out of the closet and dumped their contents onto the floor. What was he going to need? Magic Markers. Glue. Cloth. Cotton. Yarn. Fancy papers. Little boxes or baskets. What about colored tissue paper? feathers? glitter? beach glass? tempera paint? watercolors? crayons? colored pencils? sealing wax? What about this leftover Easter egg dye? Then he took the art supplies into the family room, where he arranged all the things he thought he might use on a big table. Then, for the pleasure of doing it, he rearranged them all again.

Edward saw he had five different colors of glitter: gold, silver, red, blue, and iridescent. If it were up to him, he would sprinkle a bit of glitter on everything. He wondered whether he'd be able to convince Elaine and Andrew to let him sprinkle some of it on their egg babies.

To the Rescue

"Glitter!" exclaimed Elaine. "No way!"

"Just a little?" coaxed Edward.

"No glitter," she said firmly. "I want them to look *normal*."

"Me too," said Andrew, whose egg lay on the table waiting its turn. "No glitter."

"Glitter is a dumb idea, Edward," put in Jason. That didn't surprise Edward, coming from a person who didn't appreciate a sparkly ceiling. Edward sighed and put down the tube of iridescent glitter. He picked up a black marking pen and then one of Elaine's egg babies, which he studied intently.

Charley was sprawled out right across the table, watching every move Edward made. He picked up the tube of iridescent glitter when Edward put it down. Automatically, Edward set down his pen, took the tube away from Charley, and put it out of his reach.

Now Edward went back to studying Elaine's egg. He scrutinized it until he had a clear image of the sort of face he wanted it to have. He kept in mind that he was going to have to make the other egg look exactly like this one. Nothing too fancy, he cautioned himself silently.

With his black marker, he drew ovals for eyes. Inside the ovals, he colored black circles. Now, when he looked at the egg, he had the feeling it was looking back at him.

"That's good, Edward," encouraged Elaine, who was peering over his shoulder as he worked.

"Cool," said Andrew.

"I could do that," Charley said.

"How do you know you could?" Elaine asked. "You can't even see the face from there."

"I just know I could," said Charley.

"Yeah, right," said Jason.

Edward wasn't paying attention to any of this. He was concentrating on his work.

He drew the nose. Two black dots. That was enough. He put down the black marker and picked up a red one. A tiny, slightly upturned

35

line, and the egg baby had a mouth. He didn't make the mouth smiling, but somehow by giving it just the right tilt, he made it pleasant-looking.

"That's really good, Edward," said Elaine. "I like her better already. Now do the other one, and then we can do their hair and clothes and make a basket for them to sleep in."

Edward set the egg baby down on a piece of cotton so it wouldn't roll, and picked up the blank-faced twin.

Now he concentrated even harder. This one had to look exactly like its sister, or they wouldn't be identical.

Edward started to draw the oval eyes. Elaine, Andrew, and Jason watched intently. Could Edward really make the faces identical?

The ovals looked right. Now they watched him color in the circles. Yes. Perfect! And the nose, two dots, exactly the same. The mouth. That would be harder. Would he be able to get the exact right tilt to that tiny line, so both twins would have the same mouth?

Without taking his eyes off the egg, Edward put down the black pen and groped around on the table for the red one. He picked it up and brought it close to the egg. Then he decided to take another look at the first egg.

It was then that Edward and the others realized that Charley had slipped away. And that the first egg twin was missing!

"Charley's gone!" Andrew exclaimed.

"My egg baby's gone!" cried Elaine.

Practical Jason rushed off to look out the back door. The yard was empty. "Not out in back," he reported.

All four kids flew down the hall and out the front door. And there was Charley, standing on his own lawn holding Elaine's baby none too carefully on the flat-open palm of one hand.

"Charley, you give that back to me!" Elaine commanded.

Her voice seemed to activate Charley. He began to skip in circles with the hand holding the egg raised up over his head.

"Be careful!" called Andrew. That made Charley stop skipping in circles and run in figure eights instead, still holding the egg up in the air. The green, red, and purple lights in his shoes blinked wildly.

Jason took action. He tore across the grass and lunged at Charley. "Don't, Jason! He'll drop the egg!" cried Elaine, too late.

But Charley sidestepped Jason and continued running his figure eights. At the top of his voice

he sang, "Run, run as fast as you can, you can't catch me, I'm the—um, I'm the—egg baby man!"

Jason slouched back to the front steps, where Elaine, Andrew, and Edward were trying to decide what to do.

When he saw nobody was going to chase him, Charley stood still and watched. As he watched, he absentmindedly rolled the hard-boiled egg from one hand to the other.

"We'll have to surround him," Andrew whispered, "and then all move in at once."

"Too dangerous for my egg," said Elaine. "I think we should call his mother."

"I'm with Andrew," said Jason, ready for action. "We'll surround him, and then I'll give the signal, and we'll all rush at him at the same time. He won't know which one of us is planning to tackle him, so he won't know which way to go."

"Yeah," Andrew agreed. "He'll stand there trying to decide which way to go, and one of us will swoop in and grab the egg."

"I don't know . . ." said Elaine.

"It's the only way," coaxed Jason.

Charley watched and edged closer, trying to hear what they were plotting.

"I don't think anything like that will be necessary," said Edward quietly. "I think I can handle this."

"By yourself?" asked Elaine.

"By myself," he replied.

"Sure," said Jason sarcastically, rubbing his elbow where he'd hurt it skidding on the grass.

"By myself," said Edward firmly.

"Go ahead and try," Andrew said. "And if it doesn't work, then we'll surround him. Okay?"

"Okay," said Elaine doubtfully.

"All right," Jason agreed.

"It'll work," said Edward.

"What about my egg?" Elaine wanted to know.

"It'll be perfectly safe," Edward assured her.

"Go ahead, then," Elaine said. "Before he gets restless and does something dumb."

"Before he gets hungry and does something smart!" said Jason, remembering that they were trying to rescue a hard-boiled egg.

Andrew laughed. Elaine didn't.

Edward walked toward Charley.

"Charley," Edward said in a genuinely kind voice, "rub your belly."

Charley chuckled and rubbed his belly.

"Stand on one leg."

Charley stood on one leg.

"Shake like jelly."

Charley jiggled all over, laughing.

"Now give me the egg."

He handed Edward the egg.

"Thanks," said Edward. He turned and strolled back toward the steps, where the other kids stood, looking amazed.

Charley came cheerfully along behind Edward. "What'll we do next?" he asked.

"Forget 'next,' " advised Jason.

"Beat it," answered Andrew.

"Go home," said Elaine.

Edward thought. Then he said, "Charley, you go to your house and get your mom to cook a hard-boiled egg for you. After it's cool, bring it over, and you can draw a face on it and dress it up. You can have your own egg baby. Deal?"

"It's a deal, *orange peel*!" cried Charley, lighting out for home.

" "Bye," Edward answered.

" 'Bye, *fly*!" Charley called.

Back into the family room went Edward and the others. Elaine examined her egg and saw that it was okay. She handed it to Edward. He studied it, set it down, and picked up his red marking pen and the other egg.

Carefully, he drew a mouth onto the twin.

The mouths were just alike.

41

A Jumping Frog Contest

One year in the fall, around Hallowe'en, Ms. Bascombe, the fifth-grade teacher, read "The Legend of Sleepy Hollow" out loud to anyone in school who was interested in listening. She read after school, in the multipurpose room. The story about the headless horseman inspired some scary Hallowe'en costumes. And the reading was such a success, Ms. Bascombe declared it would be a yearly event.

At Christmastime, Mr. Farrell, the assistant principal, who liked to read aloud too, read parts of *A Christmas Carol* by Charles Dickens.

Another popular yearly event was begun.

Then in the spring, when the deep voices of

bullfrogs could be heard in the evenings coming from nearby Shaw Park Lake, Mr. Fortney, who sometimes taught one grade and sometimes another, read "The Celebrated Jumping Frog of Calaveras County" by Mark Twain. And that became a yearly event, too.

Mr. Fortney always read the story so humorously even some of the kids who had graduated and gone on to middle school would come back to hear him read it again.

This spring, on the afternoon Mr. Fortney was going to read, the multipurpose room was packed. Kids were all over the place. Marlene sat behind her sister Marilyn, combing and braiding her hair. Jason and his friends Lucas Larraby and Arnie Pollack and some other middle-school boys sat leaning against the back wall with their big outdoor jackets on and their heavy backpacks on the floor beside them.

Edward sat cross-legged on the rug near the front. He sat as close to Emily Han as he could without her noticing. And Charley sat as close as he could to Edward without Edward noticing. Another first-grader, Manny Benson, sat next to Charley. Manny sat as close as he could to Charley without Charley noticing.

But just as Mr. Fortney was putting a chair up

front so he could sit down while he read, Charley did notice how close to him his friend Manny was sitting. He took off his baseball cap and whacked Manny on the head with it. "Move over," he said.

Manny took off *his* baseball cap and whacked Charley on the head with it. "You move over," he replied.

For a few seconds the two first-graders slapped at each other with their baseball caps. Then Manny got up on his knees so he could hit his friend harder. He lost his balance and toppled over. He fell onto Charley. Charley fell sideways onto Edward. And if Edward hadn't been able to brace himself quickly, he would have ended up in Emily's lap.

"Quit it!" Edward shoved Charley away.

"Yeah, quit it!" Charley shoved Manny away.

"Me quit it?" Manny objected as he moved over and put his cap back on his head.

Mr. Fortney didn't know either of the first-graders by name. So after he sat down in the straight-backed chair with the book open on his lap, ready to begin reading, he frowned at Edward. "Well, Edward, as soon as you get through roughhousing, we can begin," he said.

"Me?" said Edward.

"Shhhh," warned Emily.

"Shhhh," said Manny and Charley.

"Me?" pantomimed Edward, pointing to his chest and rolling his eyes.

"Shhhh," hissed Marlene and Marilyn.

"Beeee quiii-et!" roared Lucas.

"Ahem." Mr. Fortney cleared his throat. And he began to read Mark Twain's story about the gifted, modest, and straightforward frog named Dan'l Webster—the celebrated jumping frog of Calaveras County—and what happened to him in a jumping frog contest way back in the Gold Rush days in the state of California.

Everyone loved the story. They clapped at the end, and some of the older boys put their first and fourth fingers into their mouths and whistled loudly. Edward had been trying to learn to whistle like that, but he couldn't do it. His brother, Jason, couldn't, either. But Jason didn't care.

After the reading was over, a big group of kids headed home in the same direction. Marlene and Marilyn rode their scooters, and the rest of the kids jostled and poked one another, trying not to get shoved off the sidewalk onto the grass.

Charley was especially determined to stay on the sidewalk. Every time his foot touched the grass, he put his head down and butted someone much bigger than he was so he could get back onto the sidewalk. But every time he got back, he was shoved aside again.

"Give it up, Charley," Edward advised him. "That's life."

"What's life?" Charley wanted to know.

"That the bigger kids get to walk on the sidewalk," explained Edward.

"You're a bigger kid," Charley observed, "and you're not walking on the sidewalk."

"I'm not a bigger enough kid," explained Edward, squinching his eyes at the older, taller boys, his brother among them, who marched along as if they owned the entire sidewalk and everything else.

Charley looked up at Edward. "Well, you're a lot bigger than I am," he concluded. "When I'm as big as you are, I'm gonna walk on the sidewalk."

Edward sighed. "You probably will," he agreed.

Kids turned off as they got to their streets or to their houses. Soon the Conroys and the Frasers, Charley, and Alexander Friedman were the only ones left.

Suddenly Charley cried, "Hey, look at me! I'm a frog!"

He crouched down and then jumped up, leaping so high you'd think he had springs in his legs. The other kids had never seen anyone do that before. They stopped to watch.

Charley did it again.

"I can do that," said Alexander, who was famous for being a super athlete.

"Go ahead," said Marilyn.

"Let's see," said Marlene.

Alexander crouched on the grass. Charley sprang back to the group to see what was going on.

Alexander heaved himself up into the air—about an inch.

Charley laughed. "No," he said, "like this. Look."

He crouched down next to Alexander, and then, on his springy legs, he leaped into the air again. "See?" he said. Alexander tried again. He didn't do any better than he had the first time.

"Let me try," said Edward. He crouched down. He heaved. He grunted. He struggled. But like poor Dan'l Webster after he'd been secretly filled up with birdshot, Edward couldn't get himself off the ground at all.

Charley seemed surprised. "Watch me, Edward," he said, and off he bounced.

The kids looked at one another, shrugged, and walked on. Charley leaped on ahead until he came to his own house, and then he leaped up his front walk, " 'Bye!" he called.

Edward and Jason started up their front walk. The Conroys sped away on their scooters. And Alexander zoomed off in the direction of his own house.

Mrs. Fraser was standing out on the Frasers' front porch, watering the succulents. She was still wearing the huge shoes she wore to her Be-A-Clown class, and she had white makeup all over her face and black makeup around her eyes that made her look surprised and sad all at once.

The boys walked past her into the house. Edward took off his jacket and dropped his backpack onto the floor, where someone might trip on it. He crouched down in the hallway and closed his eyes, so he could focus on feeling like a frog. Then, with all his strength, he tried to leap forward. But again, like Dan'l Webster after the stranger tricked him, Edward couldn't budge.

"Give it up," advised Jason. "That kid's got springs in his legs instead of bones."

Edward tried two more times. Then he stretched out on the floor in the hallway so he could think.

When his mother came in, she had trouble stepping over him in her huge clown shoes. "So how was your day?" she asked, carefully putting one enormous foot and then the other over her lying-down son.

"Fine," Edward grumbled.

"That's nice, dear," she replied, waddling toward the kitchen. "Mine was, too. I practiced getting in touch with my sad clown and my silly clown."

"Your sad clown? Your silly clown?" asked Edward, turning over onto his stomach and propping his chin up on one hand.

"Yep," she answered as she waddled slowly on. "The clowns within."

"Within?"

"Within me," she explained.

"Oh," said Edward. He got up, picked up his backpack, and went to his room. "The clowns within," he pondered, wondering—not for the first time—what in the world his mother was talking about, and why she'd decided to take up clowning, anyway.

Two days later, flyers were stuck into mailboxes and stapled to telephone poles all over the neighborhood. "Jumping Frog Contest!" the flyers announced. "The First Annual Mark Twain Memorial Jumping Frog Contest!"

The contest was to be held one week from Saturday in the Conroys' back yard. It would cost fifty cents to enter. It would be just like the one Mark Twain wrote about in his story. Each frog would have a chance to jump, and the one that jumped farthest would be the winner. Whoever had the winning frog would get a prize. And the prize was a secret.

"Tune in to KIDNEWS," the flyer instructed, "for up-to-the-minute information."

KIDNEWS was Marilyn and Marlene's older sister Janice's especially-for-kids radio news show. It was on every weekday afternoon for five minutes at 4:55. At the end of the show, people could call in with questions and comments.

"Those Conroys," said Mrs. Fraser as she read the flyer, which was printed on bright yellow paper. "Look how cleverly they've used different kinds of type." She showed the flyer to Mr. Fraser.

"Enterprising, those girls," said Mr. Fraser.

"And good at making flyers," said Edward.

"They make enough of them," remarked Jason.

Edward studied the flyer. "I could make one

like this," he said, thinking about the different kinds of type he could use on his and Jason's computer.

"You could make a better one," said Jason loyally.

"Think so?" asked Edward.

Jason studied the flyer. "Sure," he said. "You could probably figure out a way to draw pictures of frogs jumping around in the margins."

Edward liked that idea. "I think I'll give it a try," he said.

"Give what a try?" asked his mother, who had not been paying attention.

"I'm going to try to make a flyer like this one with pictures of frogs in the margins. On the computer."

"Can you do that?" she asked.

"I think so," replied Edward. "If I can't, I can draw them on by hand."

"What's the point?" Mr. Fraser wanted to know. "The flyers are already made."

"That's true," Edward agreed. "But I still want to see if I can do one with frogs."

"I wonder where people will get the frogs," said Mrs. Fraser.

"Plenty of bullfrogs in Shaw Park Lake," Mr. Fraser pointed out.

"I don't think that'll work, Dad," said Jason.

"Why not?"

"Since Edward found that alligator in the lake last year, nobody's allowed to put any kind of animal into it."

"I wasn't talking about putting frogs *into* the lake, Jason," his father explained. "I was talking about taking them *out.*"

Edward had stopped to listen. "Yeah, Jas," he put in, "there's no law against taking animals out."

"Well," Jason said, talking to Edward as if Edward were a baby, "if you take a frog out of the lake to enter it in the jumping frog contest, what are you going to do with it after the contest is over?"

"What?" Edward asked.

"What?" said Jason, no longer pretending. "What? That's what I'm asking you. If you take it out of the lake, you have to put it someplace when the contest is over. And it's against the law to put it back into the lake."

"Good point, Jason," said Mr. Fraser, opening the newspaper. "I forgot about the rule they made after that alligator business. I wonder what the Conroys have in mind."

"Oh," said Mrs. Fraser, tilting her head so

her black, rhinestone-studded cat's-eye glasses sparkled in the light, "I bet the enterprising Conroys have thought of everything, including a way to solve that problem."

"I bet they have," Jason grumbled.

"I bet they have, too," agreed Edward cheerfully. "But how?"

"We can listen to the replay of KIDNEWS later on tonight," said Jason. "That's probably where we can get that 'up-to-the-minute' information."

Jason was right.

At 7:55, he and Edward sprawled on Edward's unmade bed to listen to the replay of KIDNEWS.

"This is Janice Conroy for KIDNEWS with an important announcement. A frog jumping contest, open to one and all—one and all with frogs, that is—will be held on Saturday the seventeenth at noon in the Conroy back yard at 29 College Circle. The jumping frog contest will be modeled on the original contest written about by the famous American author Mark Twain. The jumps will be measured by Mr. Z., popular Fairmount Middle School science teacher. And the contest will be judged by Mr. Fortney—this year a fourth-grade teacher—at the Bellevue Grammar School. Yours truly, Janice Conroy, will be the announcer and the mistress of ceremonies. The proceedings will be taped for broadcast in the near future on a special segment of KIDNEWS.

"A prize, still a closely kept secret at the time of this report, will be awarded to the person whose frog jumps farthest.

"Well, all of you out there in KIDNEWS-land, this sounds like an exciting event.

"We have about a minute left. Call me, Janice Conroy, right now with questions or comments. The number, as always, is 510-KIDNEWS.

"And here's our first caller, Judy. Hello? Hello? Judy? Are you on the line?"

"Hi, Janice," said a voice that sounded familiar.

"Judy?" said Jason.

"Marilyn," answered Edward. "Or Marlene."

"Shhh," said Jason.

"What's your question, Judy?" asked Janice.

"Well, you know, there are a lot of bullfrogs living in Shaw Park Lake," said "Judy," "and I want to know if it's okay to catch one of those for the contest."

"Good question, Judy. I'm glad you brought that up. It's all right to catch one for the contest. But according to Amendment 244, Section 1, of the City Code, it's not all right to put it back."

"Oh!" said "Judy" in what was clearly a fake cry of surprise.

" 'Oh!' " mimicked Jason.

Edward giggled.

"Then how can I get a frog I can enter in the contest?" the caller asked.

"Let's see, now," said Janice, "I have that information right here someplace. Oh yes. If you want to know how to get a jumping frog to enter in the contest, you can e-mail the Conroys at gogetters@fireandwater.net. Or you can stop by at the entrance to the park any day after school this week, as well as Saturday and Sunday from noon to four o'clock. Marlene and Marilyn Conroy, the contest's sponsors, will be there to give information about *renting* frogs and to sign up people who want to participate in the contest. That answer your questions, Judy?"

"Yes. Thanks, Janice," said "Judy."

"You're very welcome. And that brings us to the end of another edition of KIDNEWS. Tune in tomorrow for more fast-breaking news of special interest to kids. You'll hear it first, from me, Janice Conroy, at KIDNEWS."

"You can take them out," said Edward, "but you can't put them back."

"Told you," said Jason.

"Rats!" said Edward.

"Don't worry," Jason said. "You can always get

your pal Charley a frog costume and enter him. He'd win for sure."

"Charley?" asked Edward. "Do you think he'd win?"

"Do I think he'd win? Hands down," answered Jason.

"Frog costume," mused Edward.

Jason stood up. He looked at his brother. "We're joking, Edward," he reminded him.

Edward gazed dreamily up at the ceiling of his room, which his mother had painted with the same sparkly paint she'd used on the ceiling in the family room. He didn't answer. "We-are-joking-Edward," said Jason firmly.

"Mmmm," Edward agreed.

"Okay," said Jason as he left to get started on his two thousand hours of middle-school homework.

Want to Hear Some Frog Jokes?

The next day after school, kids headed toward the entrance to Shaw Park. Marlene and Marilyn had raced to the park the minute school was out. Their sister, Janice, met them there and helped them set up an information booth. When the others arrived, there were the Conroy twins, ready and waiting.

Charley's mother said he could go to the park if he went with Edward, and if Edward promised to keep track of him.

Edward promised.

She gave them each an oatmeal cookie and told

them to be sure to be home before it started to get dark.

Edward munched his cookie thoughtfully. Charley swallowed his in about one gulp—like a frog swallowing a fly—and instead of walking alongside Edward, he jumped like a frog.

It was bad enough for Edward to be seen after school with a weird first-grader. But to be seen with one leaping like a frog was unacceptable.

Edward stood still until Charley noticed and leaped back to where he was standing. "Charley," Edward said quietly, "flap your arms and spin around." Charley giggled, flapping and spinning. "Now walk next to me, with your feet on the ground."

Charley made a face. But he could tell Edward was serious. "And walk like a normal person, or I'll take you home and tell your mom that I'm not going to look after you."

Charley frowned.

"Walk," Edward said.

Charley took on an aggressive karate pose. "Hi-*ya!*" he cried.

"Like a normal person!" hollered Edward.

"You don't need to yell," scolded Charley.

"Sorry," said Edward.

"Okay," Charley said. "But don't do it again."

Edward spluttered.

"What?" Charley asked.

"Nothing," muttered Edward. "Just keep walking. We want to get there before the Conroys leave."

"Right," said Charley agreeably. "We do."

Marlene and Marilyn sat behind the booth they usually used when they sold lemonade or gave haircuts. Marlene sat at one end with a sign-up sheet for kids who wanted to enter the contest. Next to the sign-up sheet was a large jar with a hole punched in the lid for collecting the fifty-cent entry fees.

At the other end sat Marilyn with a sign-up sheet for kids who wanted to rent frogs in advance. Next to her sign-up sheet was a large jar with a hole punched in the lid for collecting the one-dollar frog-rental fees.

"Wait a minute," complained Andrew. "I didn't know we had to bring money ahead of time."

"And I didn't know it was going to cost so much," said Alexander.

"Me neither," said Elaine.

"Me neither," said Emily and Tyler and Rudy and some other kids.

"Calm down," said Marlene.

"Relax," said Marilyn.

"We'll be here tomorrow," said Marlene.

"And Saturday and Sunday," added Marilyn. "And every afternoon after school next week. We'll be more than happy to collect your money then."

"And to answer your questions," Marlene added quickly.

"And to take your advance orders for frogs," said Marilyn.

"Bullfrogs straight from Calaveras County, which is why renting them is a little on the expensive side," Marlene added.

"Calaveras County, where the very first jumping frog contest was held," put in Marilyn.

"Some of the frogs will probably be the great-great-great-great-great-great-grandchildren of old Dan'l Webster himself!" added Marlene.

"Maybe all of them will be!" declared Marilyn.

The rental frogs would be collected by the girls' father and their uncle, Mr. Clark, who owned a pet store, on the day before the contest.

The frogs would be fed and kept moist and watched over by Mr. Clark, who knew everything about animals. He would deliver them, ready to jump, *eager* to jump, to the Conroys' back yard two hours before the contest began.

Everyone who paid in advance would get their frogs first. People who paid at the gate would have to take the leftover ones, if there were any. But whoever rented a frog ahead of time would be sure to have one waiting and ready to jump its heart out on the day of the contest. The twins promised.

"Can we choose the one we want?" asked Tyler.

"Sure," said Marilyn.

"Of course," echoed Marlene.

"What if two people choose the same frog?" Jenny Barnes wanted to know.

"Mr. Z. will toss a coin," Marlene answered. "Mr. Z. is in charge of rules. And measuring."

"You don't have to worry," said Marilyn. "Marlene and I have thought of everything."

"Have you thought of what you're going to do with all those frogs after the contest?" hollered Arnie Pollack.

"We most certainly have," said Marlene and Marilyn.

"What?" he challenged.

"They're going to be returned to the pond," said Marilyn.

"Or to the lake," added Marlene.

"Where they came from," Marilyn finished.

Marlene squinched her eyes at Arnie. "What

else would you think we'd do with them?" she asked.

"Just checking," said Arnie.

"You didn't for one minute think we'd consider putting them back anyplace else except where they came from, did you?" asked Marlene.

"Did you?" echoed Marilyn.

"Naw," said Arnie out loud. Under his breath he said, "Not with your dad and Mr. Clark in on it, anyway."

Kids who had brought money with them signed up right then and there. Others said they would have to come back the next day. A few decided they would just watch the contest. "It would make me nervous to enter a frog in a contest," said Elaine.

"You just don't want to have to touch one!" teased Rudy.

Truthful Elaine blushed. She couldn't deny it. "But it would make me nervous, too," she said.

Edward and Charley didn't have any money with them. They would have to come back. Or pay at the gate and take their chances on getting a good jumper on the day of the contest. "Let's walk around the lake one time before we go home," Charley said. "Let's look for frogs."

The boys walked slowly. Edward kept his eyes on the water. He remembered the day he'd seen the abandoned baby alligator and all the fuss that had caused. Now there was no way he could cause a fuss. He was just trying to see a frog. And, unlike alligators, frogs were *supposed* to be living in Shaw Park Lake.

Charley picked up a stick and dragged it behind him. Edward looked all around. He knew it would be hard to see a frog unless one moved. Frogs were decorated to fit in with their environment.

He said that to Charley.

"What's environment?" Charley wanted to know.

"Where they live," said Edward.

"I know," said Charley.

"Then why'd you ask?"

"To see if you knew," Charley lied. "Want to hear a frog joke?"

Charley had never told Edward a joke that Edward hadn't heard before. But Edward had been too kind to mention it. "Sure," Edward said, sighing.

"Um," said Charley, trying to remember the joke, "oh yeah. What did the frog say to the waiter who brought him some soup?"

"Waiter, there's no fly in my soup," said Edward, who was not feeling as kind as usual.

Charley guffawed. "That's a good one, isn't it?" he said. Then he stopped laughing. "Wait a minute. How did you know?"

"I've heard that one before."

"Oh." Charley seemed very disappointed. Edward felt guilty.

They walked along in silence. "I'll teach you a new frog joke," offered Edward finally.

"You will?" Charley perked up.

"Sure," said Edward. "What does a frog eat with its hamburgers?"

"Frogs don't eat hamburgers, you silly," said Charley.

"This is a joke, Charley, remember?"

"Oh, right. What does a frog eat with its hamburgers? Hmmm," said Charley. "Don't tell me, don't tell me. Ummm. I know! Ketchup!" he cried, grinning.

"Ketchup?" said Edward. "Is that funny? The answer to a joke is supposed to be funny."

"I think it's funny," said Charley. "Hahahaha," he fake-laughed. "Ketchup!"

Edward squinched his eyes at Charley. He didn't say anything. They kept on walking along the path that went around the lake.

"What *does* a frog eat with its hamburgers, Edward?" asked Charley after a while.

"Forget it," said Edward.

"Pleeeeease," Charley begged.

"Okay, okay," said Edward. "It eats *french flies.*"

"French flies?" puzzled Charley. "I don't get it."

"You know, like hamburgers and french fries," said Edward. Charley looked blank. "Frogs eat flies. So they eat hamburgers and french *flies.*"

"That's not funny," Charley said.

"It is too," said Edward.

"Not to me it isn't," said Charley.

"You don't know what's funny," cried Edward, making up his mind never to be kind to Charley again.

Charley laughed. "You're funny, Edward," he said good-naturedly.

Edward fumed.

"What does a bullfrog look like, anyway?" Charley asked, looking at the water.

"Green on top," said Edward, "so they blend in with everything around them."

"It's not easy being green," said Charley. Edward stuck his hands deep into his pockets and sighed. "Well, it's not," said Charley. Edward didn't answer. He hummed under his breath and pretended he wasn't listening. They walked along in silence, keeping their eyes on the water.

"How far can a bullfrog jump?" Charley asked.

"I'm not sure," answered Edward, kneeling down to tie his shoe.

"How do they eat the flies? What else do they eat?" asked Charley. "How do they breathe? What do they feel like? How come they're such good jumpers? How long can they stay out of the water? How can you make a frog jump, anyway? Huh? Edward? Huh?"

Edward couldn't answer any of Charley's questions. "I don't know," he admitted. Charley looked sad. "Don't take it so hard," Edward advised. "All you need to do is go to the public library and get a book about frogs. It will tell you everything you want to know. It will probably tell you a lot more than you want to know."

"Do you think the library has a book about frogs, Edward?" asked Charley.

Edward pictured all the books in the children's room at the library. He pictured the overflowing shelves in the science section. "I'm sure it does," he said.

"When can we go, Edward?"

"Where?"

"To the library."

"We?"

"Don't you want to know the answers, too?"

Actually, now that Edward thought about it, he did. "My dad would take us over after dinner," said Edward, thinking out loud. "Except the library isn't open tonight. Why don't we try the school library tomorrow at lunchtime?"

The school library was a converted storage room, small and dark and nowhere near as nice as the public library. The school librarians were fifth-graders who volunteered to work there for extra credit. Still, the room was full of books. It would be worth a try.

"Okay." Charley smiled. He crouched down and leaped here and there, making croaking sounds.

It was getting chilly. "Time to go home," Edward announced.

"But you haven't seen a frog yet!" said Charley.

"We can't stay out all night," said Edward. "Besides, we're going to be seeing lots of frogs soon."

Charley leaped in a circle around Edward. "I don't want to go home yet," he said.

"Oh, come on, Charley," coaxed Edward. "Stop hopping around and walk home with me." Edward saw that Charley would have to be bribed. "I'll tell you a whole bunch of frog jokes on the way."

Charley was at his side in half a second.

They walked together toward the entrance to the park, past the deserted sandbox, past the swings, past the table where Mr. Han and Mr. Chan met to play chess. Past the spot where the Conroys' table had been.

"Okay," Edward said as they left the park. "Um, what does a frog with long ears say?"

"I don't know," said Charley, "what?"

"Rabbit! Rabbit!" said Edward. That cracked Charley up.

"What does a robber frog say?" said Edward.

"I don't know," said Charley, "What?"

"Rob it! Rob it!" said Edward. That cracked Charley up.

"What does a mechanical frog say?" said Edward.

"I don't know," said Charley, "what?"

"Robot! Robot!" said Edward. That cracked Charley up.

"What does a frog welder say?" said Edward.

"I don't know," said Charley, "what?"

"Rivet! Rivet!" said Edward. That cracked Charley up.

"What does a frog tailor say?" said Edward.

"I don't know," said Charley, "what?"

"Rip it! Rip it!" said Edward. That cracked Charley up.

"That's it," said Edward. "Those are all the frog jokes I know." Actually, Edward knew a few more, but he decided to hang on to them in case of an emergency.

"Well, I know another one," Charley said brightly.

"You do?"

"Yep. I just made it up out of my own head," Charley bragged. "What does a regular frog say?"

"I don't know," said Edward, "what?"

"Ribbit! Ribbit!" said Charley. And that cracked him up most of all.

"Ribbit, ribbit," muttered Edward.

"Ribbit! Ribbit!" cried Charley, laughing his head off and leaping all around. "Ribbit! Ribbit!"

The Secret

The next day at lunch recess, Edward and Charley went to the school library. The door was open, but whatever fifth-grader was supposed to be working there was missing. Nobody was sitting behind the battered old desk. Edward hesitated. He wasn't sure they should go in.

"All we're going to do is look at books," reasoned Charley, who didn't know the rules and didn't care about them. "Come on."

Edward followed him into the small, book-filled room. He found a book called *Bullfrogs*, and they both sat down on the floor to look at it.

The book was old and had a friendly feeling to it. Edward could tell that a lot of kids had read it before them. It had good, clear drawings of the outsides and the insides of bullfrogs, and not too many words. He and Charley would be able to find out everything they wanted to know about frogs before lunch recess was over.

" 'All frogs are amphibians,' " Edward read. Charley leaned over him to look at the pictures. "That means they can live both in water and on land.

" 'They have long, muscular back legs, and they are good jumpers. A bullfrog can measure up to six inches long and often can jump twenty times the length of its body.' " Edward multiplied. "Twenty times six," he said, "that's a hundred and twenty inches." Then he divided. "That's ten feet! Wow!"

"How far is ten feet, Edward?" Charley wanted to know.

"It's more than twice as far as you are tall," Edward answered.

"Wow!" said Charley.

Edward went back to the book. " 'A bullfrog has a short, squat body,' " he read, " 'no tail, and moist, green skin. A frog has no ribs, so when you hold it, it feels soft-bellied.' "

"And slimy," added Charley.

"It doesn't say slimy."

"It should."

Edward continued reading. " 'The frog's smooth, slippery skin'—"

"Slimy skin," interrupted Charley. Edward gave Charley a shut-up look. He began again.

" 'The frog's smooth, slippery skin' "—he paused; Charley was silent—" 'lets water and air in and out, so frogs have to stay moist.' "

"Moist?" asked Charley.

"Wet," said Edward.

"So how can you have a jumping contest with frogs that are away from the water?" Charley wanted to know.

"Ummm," said Edward. "Well, you could keep your frog in a bucket with some water at the bottom," he said, "at least for a while."

"You could spray it with water," suggested Charley.

"Good idea," said Edward.

"I'll borrow a spray bottle from my mom," Charley said. "Then I'll keep spraying our frog so it'll be wet and ready to really jump."

"Our frog?" said Edward.

"Yeah," Charley said, smiling. "The frog we're going to enter in the frog jumping contest."

"We?"

Charley nodded.

74

Edward thought hard. "I—um—I thought you'd want to enter your own frog, Charley," he said.

"Nope," said Charley. "I want us to enter one together. I want us to be partners. You want to be partners, don't you, Edward?"

There was something in Charley's face that made Edward say, "Um—sure." He was sorry the second the word left his mouth.

"That's what I thought," Charley said happily.

"Mmmm," grumbled Edward. He continued to read.

Bullfrogs were green on top, the book said, so if you saw them from the top or the sides, they would blend in with the greenery around them. But they were light—almost white—underneath, so if you saw them from below, they would blend in with the light-looking water above. If an enemy was above, the frogs would be protected. And if an enemy was below, the frogs would be protected, too.

"And some of them are reddish on top and red underneath, too," said Charley knowingly.

"That's not what the book says, Charley."

Charley lay down and put his arms under his head. He looked up at Edward. "But that's what color the one I saw jump out of the water yesterday at Shaw Park Lake was," he replied.

"You saw a frog jump out of the water yester-day?" Edward said. Charley nodded. "When?"

"When you were tying your shoe," said Charley.

"Like fun you did," said Edward.

"I did, Edward, really. It was dark red on top, and when it jumped, I could see that it was red underneath. And it jumped really, really far."

"You're imagining things," said Edward. Then he stopped. He remembered what everyone had said when he told them he'd seen a baby alligator in Shaw Park Lake. He remembered how he'd felt when they all said he was imagining it.

"Did you really see a red frog yesterday?" he asked.

"Yep," said Charley. "And he was a great jumper. He jumped at least three times taller than I am, I bet."

"Red underneath," mused Edward.

"And kind of red on top," Charley reminded him. "I think that made it easier to see him. I don't think he fit in all that well with his—um—"

"Environment," said Edward.

"Right," Charley said.

Edward put the bullfrog book back. He got up on his knees and scanned the shelf for other books about frogs. Ah. *Amphibians of North America*. It was a much bigger book. A kind of encyclopedia. And it was brand new. It felt stiff, and it smelled the way books smell when nobody else has read them.

Edward looked in the index. He looked under "red." Sure enough, he found an entry: "red-legged frog, 136." He turned to page 136. Charley leaned over and put his sharp chin on Edward's shoulder so he could see the book, which Edward held open on his lap.

Edward looked up from the page. "Charley," he said very quietly, "that hurts."

Charley took his sharp chin off Edward's shoulder and sat down next to him, leaning over the book so Edward couldn't see it.

"Charley," Edward said, very, *very* quietly. "I can't see the book when you sit that way."

Charley moved an eensy bit.

Quietly, "I still can't see the book."

Charley moved an eensy bit more. It was just enough. Edward sighed and looked back at the page.

" 'The red-legged frog,' " he read aloud, " 'is about four inches long. It is red-brown to gray-brown on the top and it is red underneath. The red-legged frog is the athletic amphibian made famous by Mark Twain in the short story "The Celebrated Jumping Frog of Calaveras County." ' "

"Wait a minute," said Charley. "I thought Dan'l Webster was a bullfrog."

"Yeah," said Edward thoughtfully, "so did I." He continued to read. " 'The red-legged frog, once common, is now listed as "threatened" under the Endangered Species Act of 1996.' "

"The what?"

"The Endangered Species Act," Edward explained. "It's a law that protects animals and birds and stuff when they start to disappear."

"I knew that," Charley lied.

Edward closed the book and stared into space. "Wow," he said.

"Wow?" asked Charley.

"Wow," Edward repeated. "Charley, can you keep a secret?"

"Sometimes," Charley answered truthfully. "What's the secret?"

"For now, the secret is that Dan'l Webster wasn't a bullfrog."

"I can keep that secret," said Charley.

"And the other part of the secret is that there's a red-legged frog living in Shaw Park Lake."

"I can keep that secret," said Charley.

"And that the red-legged frog is a great jumper."

Charley thought. "Yep," he decided. "I can keep all those things a secret."

"It's important," warned Edward. "Because it could help us to win the jumping frog contest."

"Really? How?"

Just then the bell rang. Lunch recess was over. They had to go back to their classrooms.

Edward got up and put the book back on the shelf. "I don't have time to tell you now. But you can't tell anyone anything about this, or we might not win. Okay?"

"Okay," said Charley soberly.

"Cross your heart?" asked Edward.

Charley crossed his heart. "I won't tell anyone, Edward. I promise."

It was impossible to know when Charley was lying.

"Good," Edward said. "Meet me at my house tomorrow morning, and I'll tell you my plan."

"Plan!" Charley repeated with satisfaction. "We have a secret. And we have a plan." He looked happy.

"But we won't have anything if you tell," Edward warned.

"I won't," Charley said. "I really, really won't."

Edward wished he could tell when Charley was lying, but he couldn't. He would just have to trust him.

"Edward." Charlie tugged on Edward's shirt. "What about today? Why don't I come over after school today so you can tell me about the plan?"

"You can't come today. You have karate today," Edward reminded him. And to himself, Edward thought, And if you came today, I'd have nothing to tell you. I have to *think* of a plan before I can tell you about it!

"What I'll do today is go over to the park and pay our entry fees," said Edward. "Do you have that fifty cents you were supposed to bring?"

Charley frowned and dug deep into the front pocket of his jeans. He came up with four dimes and handed them to Edward.

Edward waited. "Isn't that enough?" asked Charley.

"It's forty cents," Edward told him. "You need another dime."

"Do you have a dime, Edward?" Charley wanted to know.

"Yes," said Edward.

"Good," Charley said. "Then it's enough."

Charley took off down the hallway in the direction of his first-grade classroom. Edward put the four dimes into his pocket. He knew he could make Charley come up with another ten cents. But it wouldn't be worth it. He had enough money to pay his own entry fee and the rest of Charley's. And with any luck at all, they wouldn't be paying a dollar to the Conroys to rent a bullfrog.

When Edward got home, he went into the kitchen for a snack. His mother was sitting at the kitchen table with her hand mirror and, spread out on the table in front of her, her collection of false noses.

Edward poured himself a glass of orange juice.

He examined the noses, to see if she'd gotten any new ones. There was the dog nose, the cat nose, the alligator nose with the sharp white teeth. There was the snake-head nose with its fangs, the pig snout, the fish nose, the bird of prey nose, the elephant's trunk, the scary great white shark nose, and the orange and pink toucan bill nose. Nothing new.

"Same old noses," he said congenially.

"Yep," answered his mother, slipping the rubber band of the pig snout around the back of her head and picking up the mirror to study the effect.

"What do you think?" she asked Edward. "Is it me?"

"Is it *you*?" he asked. "What do you mean?"

"Is this nose the nose that suits who I am? As a clown, I mean."

"I don't know who you are as a clown, Mom," said Edward.

"Neither do I," his mother answered. "I don't know *yet*. I thought the right nose might help me figure it out."

"Try on some others," Edward said helpfully, "and let's see."

His mother tried on all the noses. Edward tried on the shark and the alligator and the dog. He and his mother handed the mirror back and forth and laughed at each other.

But it didn't do the trick. "I'm not sure any of these noses is me," concluded Mrs. Fraser.

"You could wear one of those red clown noses," suggested Edward.

"That's what all clowns wear," Mrs. Fraser replied.

"Well, maybe that's because a clown is supposed to have a clown nose," reasoned Edward.

"Maybe," his mother said. "I have to think about it. Maybe I'll just wear my makeup and take all the noses with me and use them all.

Maybe one will work one time and another will do the trick another time."

"What trick?"

"The trick of making a sick kid laugh."

"Why does the kid have to be sick?"

"Because that's why I'm learning to be a clown," Mrs. Fraser explained. "So I can go around to hospitals and clown around with sick kids and make them laugh. Laughing always makes you feel better. Some people think it can actually help you to get well."

"I wondered why you were doing this," Edward said.

"Why didn't you ask, then?" inquired his mother.

"I didn't want to be *nosy*," replied Edward.

His mother smiled as she put her false nose collection back into the plastic grocery bag where she kept it.

"What else are you going to do to make sick kids laugh?" asked Edward.

"I'm not sure yet," his mother answered. "I have to figure out a clown personality. And I have to learn clown skills."

"What kind of skills?"

"Juggling and walking on stilts and riding a unicycle. If I can."

"That's what clowns always do," said Edward.

"I know," his mother answered. "But you have to master the basics before you can do stuff that's more original."

"Like what?"

"Well, what I'm thinking of is making puppets and using them to tell stories. And having the kids use them to tell stories. That way we'll be able to talk about feelings without anybody being embarrassed."

"Feelings?"

"How it feels to be sick," his mother explained. "How it feels to be in the hospital. How it feels to miss school."

Edward nodded. He was glad he wasn't sick. Or in the hospital. Or missing school. But he liked the idea of puppets. "I'll help you make some puppets when you get around to it," he offered.

Edward and his mother had made a great puppet once. They had used a balloon and had built a head around it with strips of newspaper and flour-and-water glue. They had made a huge puppet head, and then when it was dry, they had pulled out the balloon. Then they'd attached some material for a body. And then they'd painted a face on the big, round papier-mâché head and glued on some yarn hair. They'd given it to someone for a birthday present. Edward loved the idea of making more puppets.

"Great!" said his mother. "When I get to it. But first I have to learn all the other things. And graduate from clown school, too."

"Well, when you get to the puppets, let me know," said Edward again.

"I will," Mrs. Fraser told him.

"Mom," he asked, "you know the sign they put up by Shaw Park Lake after the alligator?" Mrs. Fraser looked blank. "The sign. By the lake?" said Edward. "The sign that says 'It is against the law to put any animal into this lake.' What do you think it means?"

"The meaning doesn't seem exactly mysterious," said Mrs. Fraser. "It means what it says. It's against the law to put animals into the lake. It's against the law to dump pet turtles or fish—or alligators—into the lake when people get tired of taking care of them."

"But what if someone put something into the lake that lived there in the first place?" he asked.

"If it lived in the lake in the first place, Edward," his mother reasoned, "it would be in the lake."

Jason had come into the kitchen just in time to hear the end of the conversation. He looked knowingly at Edward, but he didn't say anything until his mother picked up her bag of noses and left. Then he said, "Thinking of putting something into Shaw Park Lake, Edward?"

"Like what?" asked Edward.

"How should I know what? Are you?"

"Of course not. Why?"

"Just wondered," said Jason.

"Wondered what?" asked Edward, trying to find out if Jason was hot on his trail or if his brother was just fishing.

"I wondered why you were suddenly so interested in that law."

"Oh, I just wanted to make sure I understood it," said Edward. "I have to explain a lot of things to Charley, you know. I don't want to give him wrong answers, so I try to double-check."

Jason looked long and hard and disbelievingly at Edward. Then he made himself a peanut butter and chocolate chip sandwich.

"I thought you were only eating healthy stuff," Edward said, changing the subject.

"Peanut butter on whole wheat bread," said Jason, waving his sandwich in Edward's direction.

"With chocolate chips," Edward reminded him.

"That's the healthy part," Jason said, pouring himself some milk.

Edward saw he'd succeeded in distracting his brother.

"I'm going over to the park to pay the Conroys for Charley and me," he announced. "Are you going to enter the contest, Jason?"

Jason shook his head no. "But I'm going to come to it and laugh my head off," he said.

"At what?" asked Edward.

"I don't know yet," said Jason. "But I know there'll be plenty of stuff to laugh at when the time comes."

Edward wanted to ask why you couldn't enter the contest and laugh at the funny stuff, too. But Jason had started reading the paper, and Edward decided to leave well enough alone.

" 'Bye," he said, heading out.

"Are you renting a frog, too?" Jason wanted to know.

"Not today. I don't have enough money," Edward lied. "I have to wait until I get my allowance. I'll rent one on the day of the contest."

"That means you'll get a leftover frog," warned Jason.

"Yep," said Edward. "Charley and I will just have to take our chances."

"Charley?" asked Jason.

"We're partners," explained Edward.

Jason rolled his eyes and went back to the paper.

Edward left for the lake.

After Edward paid the Conroys his and Charley's entry fees, he set out by himself along the path that went around Shaw Park Lake.

As soon as he rounded the first curve and was out of sight of the kids gathered around the sign-up booth, he ran as fast as he could back to the spot where he'd stopped to tie his shoe the day before. Where Charley said he'd seen a red-legged frog.

Edward left the path and crept down the grassy slope to the lake. He crouched near the water and sat as still as a stone.

He crouched as long as he could. When his legs started to hurt, he sat down on the damp grass and waited some more.

He heard someone riding a bike on the path above, and he turned to see who it was. He saw Officer Mendez ride past. Then, just as he turned his eyes back to the lake, he saw the frog. It was high in the air, in the middle of a jump. It had a reddish-brown back, it was red underneath, and it had a happy expression on its face!

Edward watched the red-legged frog land, and then jump again, land and jump again. The frog reminded Edward of Charley, jumping all over the place just for the fun of it.

Edward sat and watched until he started to feel cold and the color of the sky told him it was time for him to hurry home.

Edward had seen exactly what Charley saw: a red-legged frog, a *real* descendant of Dan'l Webster, a great jumper who could probably outjump any big old bullfrog in the contest. Would it really be against the law, Edward pondered as he headed home, to put a frog back into the lake afterward if that was where the frog came from in the first place?

He had nobody to ask without giving away his secret and his plan. He would just have to take the chance. It didn't make sense to him that it would be wrong to put something back where it came from. It seemed to him that it would be right, not wrong, to do that.

Yes, Edward decided, the important thing was that there wasn't any law at all about taking anything *out* of the lake. So the plan he'd made would work. And it wouldn't be against the law. He hoped.

"Here's the plan," Edward said to Charley the next morning as they sat on the couch watching cartoons and playing with Edward's pet rat, Spike.

Charley looked at him with shining eyes. "A secret and a plan," he said happily.

"We'll leave early to go to the jumping frog contest—but not too early, because we don't want anyone to be suspicious," said Edward, thinking about his curious brother.

"How early?" asked Charley, thinking about his watchful mother.

"About an hour before we go to the contest. Say, ten o'clock. We'll go down to the lake and see if we can catch the red-legged frog."

"How will we catch it?" asked Charley.

"With our hands," said Edward. "Carefully. We don't want to squish it."

"Squish it," chuckled Charley.

"Charley," said Edward firmly, "that is not funny."

"Yes it is," Charley said.

"No-it's-not," said Edward.

"I think it's funny," said Charley.

"What's funny about a squished frog?" cried Edward.

"Nothing!" exclaimed Charley. "It's the word that's funny! *Squished*!"

Edward felt guilty. "Oh," he said. "I thought you meant the frog."

"You silly," Charley said.

Edward went back to the plan. He would bring a plastic mop bucket to carry the frog in, and a piece of an old screen he and Jason had been saving to use when they built their tree house. They would use the screen to cover the top of the bucket so the frog couldn't jump out. They would have to bring a towel, so they could wipe themselves off if they got wet and muddy catching the frog.

"What if we don't see it?" Charley wanted to know.

"Then we can't catch it," said Edward.

"What if we see it and can't get it?" asked Charley.

"Then we can't enter it in the contest," said Edward.

"Then how will we get to be in the contest?"

"We'll have to rent a bullfrog from the Conroys."

"A rented frog will never jump like that one," Charley said.

Edward knew he was right. No other frog would jump like that one. That frog jumped for the fun of it. You could tell by the look on its face.

"Well," said Edward thoughtfully, "if we can't get that one and you don't want to rent a frog, we could dress *you* up in a frog costume and enter you. You could probably outjump any of the frogs."

"I could!" exclaimed Charley. He slid off the couch, and then he crouched and leaped, crouched and leaped, *Boing! Boing! Boing!* all around the family room.

"Charley!" cried Edward.

Charley kept leaping.

"Charley! Listen to me!"

"I'm listening!" *Boing!*

"Put your hands behind your head and stay still as a mouse!" commanded Edward.

Charley stopped leaping. He put his hands behind his head and kept very still. He looked at Edward with bright, expectant eyes, waiting for him to continue.

"Put your hands behind your head and be still as a mouse . . . um," Edward repeated, thinking hard. "Um . . . remember this rule: no frogs in the house!" he concluded, pleased with himself for coming up with a rhyme so quickly.

As always, it worked. Charley giggled. He scooted across the room on his bottom and sat next to Edward. "What's the *rest* of the plan, Edward?"

"What do you mean?" Edward asked.

"I mean after we catch the frog and enter it into the contest and it wins and we get the prize, then what will we do with the frog?"

Edward didn't answer. He didn't want to tell Charley the rest of his plan. It didn't seem fair to invite a first-grader to help him maybe break a law.

"I'll tell you when the time comes," he said.

"Tell me now," begged Charley.

"The time hasn't come yet."

"How will you know when it comes?"

"I'll know."

Charley was silent, thinking. "Are we going to put it back into the lake, Edward?"

"*We* aren't," Edward answered truthfully. "It might be against the law."

"I know that. But are we going to anyway?"

"No," said Edward, "*we* are not."

"Then what are we going to do?" Charley nagged. "The time's come, Edward. You have to tell me the rest of the plan. You have to, you have to, you have to, you have to, you—"

"Okay!" cried Edward. "Okay! Here's the rest of the plan. After we get through at the contest, *you* are going to go home and leave everything else to *me. That's* the rest of the plan."

Charley thought about this. Then he said, "Can I take the prize home with me?"

"What prize?"

"The prize we get when our frog wins the contest."

"Sure you can."

That satisfied Charley. He smiled. "Sounds like a good plan, Edward," he said.

Leap, Frog

On the Saturday morning of the jumping frog contest, Edward collected the mop bucket from the cleaning closet and an old towel from the rag bag. He got the piece of screen out of the stack of odds and ends waiting to be made into a tree house.

"What's the bucket for?" Jason wanted to know.

"Frog," said Edward.

"What frog?"

"The frog Charley and I are entering in the contest."

"I thought you didn't have enough money to rent a frog," said Jason.

"I didn't, until I got my allowance. Remember?" Edward answered.

"Mmmm," his brother replied.

" 'Bye, Mom," Edward called. "I'm going now. To the Conroys' frog jumping contest. I'm taking the mop bucket so I can keep the frog I'm going to *rent* in it. I'm going early so I can *rent* a good jumper."

" 'Bye, Edward" came his mother's voice from somewhere in the house. "Good luck!"

"Are you coming to the contest, Jason?" Edward asked on his way out.

"Yep," said Jason.

"Changed your mind about entering a frog?"

"Nope," said Jason. He tried to look Edward in the eye, but Edward wouldn't let him.

"Hope you and Charley *rent* a good jumper," Jason said finally.

"We will," Edward assured him as he left the kitchen and headed out.

Edward picked up Charley at his house. He had an empty spray bottle hooked to his belt. The two boys hurried to the park.

They didn't go anywhere near the main entrance. Instead, they approached the lake in a secret way that Edward and Jason and some of their friends knew about, slipping and sliding downhill through overgrown bushes until they came to the paved path that went around the lake.

Charley started to walk across the path, but Edward held him back. Two joggers passed. "Okay," said Edward, "now!"

The boys hurried across and down the gentle slope that brought them to the water.

"Remember," Edward told Charley, "you have to be really patient. This is going to take a long time. First we have to find the red-legged frog. That won't be easy. Then, *if* we find him, we have to catch him. And that won't be easy, either. And if we can't find him and catch him in about an hour, which probably we can't, then we'll just have to go on to the contest and rent a frog from the Conroys instead."

"There he is, Edward," Charley said, pointing. The red-legged frog was sitting on a flat rock by the side of the lake.

Before Edward could say or do anything, Charley darted over to the rock, scooped up the frog, and held him in his cupped hands. Edward stood stock still, amazed.

"Get some water in the bucket, Edward," Charley said, "so I can put him in. I can tell he doesn't like me holding him."

Edward rushed to the lakeside, took the towel and the rolled-up screen out of the bucket, scooped up some water and a little mud, and hurried over to Charley.

Charley gently slid the red-legged frog into the bucket, and Edward covered the top with the screen.

"That wasn't so hard," Charley said cheerfully.

For some reason, Edward felt grumpy. He didn't answer. Charley filled his spray bottle with lake water, and the boys left the park the usual way, by the entrance. Nobody there paid any attention to them. They weren't wet, and they weren't muddy. And it had taken about three minutes for them to catch the red-legged frog.

"See, Edward," Charley repeated, "that wasn't so hard. Edward?"

Edward was silent.

"It wasn't, was it?" nagged Charley. "Was it? Was it?"

Edward sighed. "No," he had to admit, "it wasn't."

Charley beamed.

The Conroys' back yard was full of people. A canvas tarp had been stretched across the grass, making a very large area for the frogs to jump on.

Marlene and Marilyn had set up their booth on the deck. Two big barrels with frogs in them stood nearby. A sign on one barrel said FROGS FOR RENT. A sign on the other barrel said GREAT JUMPERS PAID FOR IN ADVANCE.

Janice was setting up her equipment. She was going to announce the contest and tape it, too. She planned to replay the exciting parts on KID-NEWS.

Mr. Conroy and Mr. Clark were pulling the canvas tight and securing it to the ground with tent pegs.

Mr. Z., wearing a shiny blue athletic suit, was measuring the canvas with a large, official-looking retractable metal measuring tape. He had read up on bullfrogs, and he knew that a six-inch bull-frog might be able to jump 120 inches—ten feet! Mr. Z. wanted to be sure the official jumping area was long enough. It was two times that long. It measured more than twenty feet.

Mr. Fortney was wearing an old gray sweatshirt with a big homemade cardboard badge pinned onto it. The badge said JUDGE. He carried a clip-board and a pen. He had a retractable metal measuring tape just like Mr. Z.'s hanging on his belt. Elaine stood nearby. She wore a homemade badge that said ASSISTANT JUDGE.

The yard was quickly filling up with people. Rudy and Jeffrey and Tyler and Alexandra had all rented frogs in advance. These frogs were in brightly colored plastic buckets, loaned by the Conroys.

Marlene and Marilyn had their own frog on the deck behind their chairs. It sat, gulping, in a fancy wooden carrying case with a shiny metal handle and screened-in sides.

"What's that?" asked Marlene, when she saw Edward's brown mop bucket.

"It's a mop bucket," he answered.

"With a piece of screen over the top," said Charley.

"I can see that," Marlene replied. "What's inside it?"

"Our frog!" Charley said.

Marlene and Marilyn looked at each other. Then Marilyn said, "We didn't get paid for that frog yet, did we?"

"Of course not," said Charley, laughing.

Marlene glared at him. She stared at Edward, waiting for him to explain.

"It's not a rental frog," Edward told her. "We brought our frog with us."

"Really?" said Marlene and Marilyn, leaning over the table to look into the mop bucket.

"Small," sniffed Marlene, after she studied the red-legged frog.

"Puny," her sister agreed.

"Are you sure you don't want to rent one of ours?" Marlene asked.

"We've got a couple of really good jumpers left," Marilyn added. "Take a look, why don't you?"

Edward peeked into the frog-rental barrel. He saw several large bullfrogs sitting on the bottom.

"We'll stick with the one we brought," he told the girls.

"Okay," said Marlene, shaking her head to show him how foolish she thought his decision was.

Everyone who was entering the contest chose numbers out of a box Mr. Fortney passed around. Edward and Charley ended up last. Marlene and Marilyn were first.

"And now," said Janice into the microphone, "the First Annual Mark Twain Memorial Jumping Frog Contest is about to begin. Judges, are you ready?"

"Ready!" called out Mr. Fortney.

"Ready," echoed Elaine.

"Rulesperson and measurer, are you ready?"

"I'm ready," declared Mr. Z.

"Okay," continued Janice. She walked onto the canvas and pointed with her foot to a piece of red duct tape that had been pasted down near one end. "This is the starting line," she explained. "Every contestant will put his or her frog down right here. If a frog does not jump by itself, the contestant can do anything he or she wants to do to make it jump—except touch it. If you touch your frog, you will be automatically disqualified.

"Let the contest begin," she said cheerfully, "and good luck to one and all!"

Marlene and Marilyn marched to the starting line, carrying their fancy frog box.

"Remember the rules," Janice repeated. "You can't touch your frog, but you can do anything else to make it jump."

Marlene slid open one screened-in side of the fancy box. Marilyn carefully took out the frog. She set it down on the starting line.

The frog squatted on the tarp with its bulgy eyes half-closed. It did not look to Edward like a frog that was interested in jumping. But he knew that Marlene and Marilyn had had first pick. And he knew they wouldn't have picked a frog that they didn't know was a great jumper.

Everyone crowded around so they could see.

The frog sat on the red-duct-tape starting line.

"It's not going to jump," someone whispered.

Just then, Marilyn knelt down behind the frog and clapped her hands sharply, right behind its head.

Instantly, the Conroys' frog threw itself through the air, pushing off with its powerful back legs and sailing much farther than anybody watching had imagined such a fat, sleepy-looking frog could possibly sail.

"Wow!" cried Charley.

A couple of the kids started to clap, and soon everyone in the back yard was applauding. You had to appreciate a frog that could jump like that.

Marlene and Marilyn stood together smiling and looking pleased as punch. Mr. Z. quickly marked the exact spot where the Conroys' frog had landed. And Mr. Clark picked up the frog and returned it to its carrying case so it couldn't hop off the tarp into the bushes.

Mr. Z. measured the distance between the starting line and the place the Conroys' frog landed. "Nine feet!" he exclaimed, shaking his head in amazement. Mr. Fortney and Elaine wrote down the number in their judges' notebooks.

The next frog was Rudy's, and it wouldn't jump at all. Rudy did everything he could think of to make it jump. He clapped his hands behind its head, the way Marilyn had. He jumped around pretending to be a frog. He shouted and hollered, he whispered and coaxed. He hopped and danced. No matter what Rudy did, his frog just sat on the tarp. It did not have jumping on its mind. It had sitting still and waiting for an insect to fly by so it could catch it and eat it on its mind.

Finally, Rudy quit making a fool of himself and gave up. "And I rented this frog in advance," he complained.

Mr. Fortney and Elaine wrote "0" in their notebooks.

Emily stepped forward and placed her frog on the starting line. As soon as it touched the tarp, it began to hop away. "Wait!" cried Emily. But the frog kept hopping.

Mr. Clark gently picked it up and returned it to the rental frog barrel. Marlene took back Emily's bucket. And Mr. Z. quickly measured the distance between the starting line and the place the frog had landed after its first hop. "Three inches," he announced.

Mr. Fortney and Elaine recorded the distance in their notebooks.

And so it went.

Some frogs refused to jump, like Rudy's.

Some hop-hopped away, like Emily's.

Some jumped, like Marlene and Marilyn's, but not nearly as far.

Finally, everyone had had their turn except Edward and Charley.

By this time, they all knew that Edward and Charley hadn't rented a frog but had brought their own. Everyone had peered down through the piece of screen and into the mop bucket to view the frog. They had all seen that it wasn't a bullfrog. And they had all listened to Charley bragging up a storm about what a great jumper his frog was.

Everybody had listened to him, but nobody had believed him. Still, they were curious, and they crowded around when Edward and Charley finally got their turn.

"Let me put him down," Charley said to Edward.

Edward hesitated.

"Please, Edward, please?" Charley begged.

Edward hesitated some more. But Charley was the one who'd spotted the frog and caught him. Fair is fair, thought Edward. "Okay," he said.

Both boys knelt at the starting line. Edward

pulled away the screen, and Charley peered into the bucket.

"Edward," Charley whispered, "he's ready to jump. He's *smiling*."

Charley reached into the bucket and gently lifted out the red-legged frog. Then he grinned at Edward, his eyes dancing with excitement.

"Watch what you're doing, Charley," Edward warned—a moment too late! Charley, not paying attention, had already accidentally lost hold of the slick amphibian, which slipped out of his hand and landed smack on the starting tape.

As soon as the frog felt the ground underneath him, he pushed off with his long, strong legs and *flew* into the air.

He flew over the heads of the watching children, over the bushes growing along the fence, and over the fence into the neighbors' back yard!

He flew in the wrong direction!

"Wow!"

"Look at that!"

"What a jump!"

"Someone go get it!"

"See where it landed!"

"Don't let it get away!"

"Hurry!"

Edward stood with his mouth open, stunned. Charley danced around, doing a frantic, excited jig.

Everyone was shouting directions at everyone else. But nobody was doing anything.

Then Jason pushed through the shrubs and scrambled over the fence. His pal Andrew went over after him.

"Be careful!" cried Edward, thinking they might jump down on the frog when they landed on the other side.

"Don't step on him!" cried Charley, thinking the same thing.

"Did you see that sucker jump?" asked Lucas, speaking to no one in particular.

Charley grinned up at Lucas. "He *loves* to jump," he told him.

Mr. Z. started measuring the distance from the starting line to the fence. He measured it along the ground.

"*Ten* feet, up to here," he told Mr. Fortney, who wrote down the number.

"But that isn't the whole jump," Elaine reminded them.

She was right. But there was no way of telling exactly where the frog had landed, explained Mr. Z., so that was as far as he could honestly measure.

"Maybe it doesn't matter," Mr. Fortney said. "Even if you measure only to the fence, this frog is still the winner by a whole foot!"

"An amazing jump, performed by entry number twenty-two," said Janice in her excited newscaster voice, speaking into her recorder. "A frog with red markings, a little guy, only about four inches long, the entry of Charley O'Hara and Edward Fraser, has just astounded the audience here at the First Annual Mark Twain Memorial Jumping Frog Contest by leaping right out of the jumping area and right out of the back yard. What a jump!" she cried. "What a jumper!"

Marlene, her face pink with anger, tugged at her sister Janice's shirt. "That jump can't be measured," she whispered. "Nobody saw it land."

Janice thought for a moment, then she nodded. "Unfortunately," she continued, in her announcer voice, "the jump cannot really be measured. The frog jumped right over the fence into the neighbors' yard. Nobody saw it land!"

Marilyn, *her* face pink with anger, shoved Marlene aside and tugged at Janice's shirt. "That doesn't matter," she whispered, "what really matters is, it jumped in the wrong direction. Even if they can figure out a way to measure the jump, it won't count. It was facing the wrong way!"

Janice thought about this for a moment. "What's more," she went on brightly, "even if they can find a way to measure what was clearly a stupendous, unusual, amazing"—the twins glared at their older sister—"um, a really *big* jump, the jump might not *count*. The frog was facing the wrong way, and it jumped in the wrong direction. A tremendous, *winning* jump"—now Janice glared at her younger sisters—"which may not be able to be measured and may not be able to be counted. Through no fault of its own, this *gifted* jumping frog, clearly the best jumper in this contest here today—and perhaps the best jumper anyone has ever seen or will ever see again—may be deprived of its victory because it accidentally faced the wrong way on the starting line!"

Jason came back into the Conroys' yard, this time through the gate, holding the red-legged frog in his cupped hands. Andrew and Mr. Z. followed after him.

"Is he okay?"
"Where was he?"
"How far did he jump?"

"Hold your horses," said Mr. Z. "Calm down. I've marked the spot where we found him, right smack in the middle of the yard next door. He was sitting there just like he'd been there all his life. But we don't have any way of knowing whether that's where he landed or whether he jumped again to get to that spot. So it wouldn't be fair to measure any part of the distance beyond the fence."

"Mr. Fortney's already measured the distance to the fence." Elaine spoke up. "And even without counting anything else, number twenty-two jumped a whole twelve inches more than any other frog in the contest anyway. Number twenty-two is the winner!"

"Says who?" Marlene asked.

"Says who?" Marilyn echoed.

Elaine, who had been concentrating on the measuring and hadn't been listening to Janice, didn't have any idea how to answer the twins. She turned to Mr. Fortney. "Isn't that true, Mr. Fortney?" she asked. "Number twenty-two outjumped all the other frogs. Doesn't that make it the winner?"

"It did outjump all the other frogs," agreed Mr. Fortney.

"But it jumped in the wrong direction," Lucas called out.

"It did jump in the wrong direction," said Mr. Fortney thoughtfully.

"But it jumped the farthest," persisted Elaine.

Edward carried the mop bucket over to his brother, and Jason slid the frog back into it. Charley sprayed the frog with water from his sprayer.

"Thanks, Jas," said Edward.

"Not a problem," Jason replied. "You guys *rented* yourselves some jumper."

Edward blushed, remembering his lie.

Now Charley got excited. He began to run around, doing circles and figure eights. "We won!" he hollered. "We won!"

"I don't *think* so!" declared Marlene.

"No way!" declared Marilyn.

"We won! We won!" screeched Charley, whirling faster and faster and faster around the yard.

Jason slipped the screen over the top of the mop bucket. Then he took the bucket from Edward. "I'll hold this," he said. "You better take care of *that*." He nodded toward Charley, now wildly leaping, hopping, whirling, and twirling.

"Charley!" called Edward loudly. "Um—fist on nose!"

Charley stopped and looked at Edward. He put his fist on his nose. "Um," said Edward. "Um—feet in the air!"

Charley laughed, fell down on his back, and waved his feet in the air.

"Now sit up straight," said Edward. Charley sat cross-legged on the tarp.

"And stay right there!"

Charley froze and stayed right where he was.

Jason handed the bucket back to Edward. "Well done," he said to his brother.

Mr. Fortney, Mr. Z., and Elaine had their heads together. They all looked serious. Marlene and Marilyn stood a little bit away from the measurer and the judges, trying to hear what they were saying to one another. Janice was talking into her machine:

"Now the judges and the official measurer are conferring. What will their decision be? Which frog will be the winner of this contest? Will it be the amazing frog that jumped the farthest, but in the wrong direction? Or will it be the other great jumper, who followed the rules to the letter and performed his excellent jump in the right direction? It's up to the judges to decide, and decide they will. I don't envy them. This is a heavy responsibility. And something nobody could have planned for.

"Who would have thought that someone would accidentally put down his frog facing the wrong way? And who could have predicted that that frog would have been the best jumper of all?

"I'm Janice Conroy, and this is KIDNEWS coming to you from the First Annual Mark Twain Memorial—wait, wait, the judges and the measurer have stopped talking. Mr. Fortney, the chief judge, is stepping to the center of the jumping tarp. He's holding up his hands for silence. I'm going to move closer to him so you can hear him announce the decision."

Janice moved closer to Mr. Fortney so his voice would be picked up by her microphone. Mr. Fortney cleared his throat and looked around the yard. Every eye was on him. Everyone was listening.

"Number twenty-two jumped the farthest," the teacher said.

"Hurray!" cried Lucas.

"Unfortunately," Mr. Fortney continued, ignoring Lucas, "number twenty-two jumped in the wrong direction, which made it impossible for the measurer to accurately and fairly measure his jump.

"Number twenty-two, therefore, sadly, has been disqualified." Mr. Fortney paused while the children groaned their objection to this decision. "And that means that the winner of today's contest is number one, the strong bullfrog that jumped a full nine feet! Let's have a round of applause for number one."

Marlene and Marilyn stepped forward, holding their fancy frog carrying case between them. Nobody clapped.

"Come on, now," Mr. Fortney coached, "rules are rules. It can't count, even if you're the best jumper, if you go in the wrong direction and nobody can measure your jump. Isn't that right?"

"But it wasn't the frog's fault!" piped Charley, still sitting cross-legged on the tarp. "It was my fault. I accidentally dropped him, and he landed on the starting line facing the wrong way. It was my fault!" Charley started to cry.

Mr. Fortney knelt down. "Don't cry," he said. "You didn't mean to drop your frog and have him face the wrong way, did you?"

Charley snuffled. "No," he answered. "You just made a mistake," Mr. Fortney said kindly. "Everybody makes mistakes, don't they?"

Charley nodded and wiped the tears off his cheeks with his dirty hands.

"I guess," he said.

"Of course they do," Mr. Fortney assured him. "We all make mistakes."

"But it wasn't the *frog's* fault!" Charley began to cry again. "Our frog was the best jumper, and he didn't win, and it was my fault, and it's not fair!"

Mr. Fortney looked around for help. Everyone watched and waited. The teacher stood up and scratched his head. "Well, it's true," he said, thinking out loud. "We have a great jumper who is losing because of a technicality."

"How about a second prize?" called out Lucas.

"Yeah," said his pal Morely.

"Yeah," said Andrew and Jason and some of the other kids. "Second prize for number twenty-two!"

The judges and Mr. Z. put their heads together again.

Janice continued describing what was going on for her listeners.

Finally, another decision was made. Number one was the first-place winner. The Conroy twins got a huge fake-gold winner's cup with "Number One!" and the date engraved on it.

Number twenty-two was the second-place winner. And as soon as it could be made, Charley and Edward would get a prize, too: a Xerox copy for each of them of Mark Twain's famous story.

The First Annual Mark Twain Memorial Jumping Frog Contest was over. Mr. Clark collected the rental frogs and put them back into the barrels. He put the barrels into his van. He and Mr. Conroy would drive them to Calaveras County that evening.

Edward knew he and Charley had to leave quickly, before anyone had a chance to ask them any questions. They took off the minute they could and made for Shaw Park Lake.

When they were about halfway there, Edward remembered his plan. "Hold on," he said. "You're not supposed to be coming with me."

"How come?" Charley wanted to know.

"Because that's not the plan, remember?"

"The plan was that I was supposed to go home with the first-place prize while you went back to the lake," said Charley. "I remember."

"Well?" said Edward.

"Well, we didn't get first place. Or any prize yet. So that's the end of the plan," said Charley. "Isn't it?"

"I guess it is," said Edward.

"It is," Charley said firmly.

"Sorry about what happened," said Charley.

"It doesn't matter," said Edward. "Our frog was the best jumper."

"That's why I'm sorry," Charley said. "We would've won if I didn't let him slip and all."

"Winning isn't everything," Edward replied.

"It's not?"

"Nope."

"How come?"

"Well, think about it. Our frog got to show what a great jumper he is. Isn't that as good as getting a fake-gold cup with 'Number One!' written on it?"

Charley thought. "I'd like the cup, too," he decided.

"Well, so would I," Edward admitted. "But we can't have it. Not this time, anyway. There's always next year, though, when we win the *Second* Annual—"

"Mark Twain Memorial Jumping Frog Contest!" finished Charley.

Nobody at the crowded park paid any attention to the boys as they marched in through the main entrance, past the baby playground, past the sun shelter where the old men were playing chess, and onto the path, crowded with in-line skaters, joggers, dog walkers, and bike riders.

Usually, Saturday afternoon wasn't a good time to walk around the lake. But today Edward was very glad to be part of the crowd. Nobody cared a bit about two boys walking along carrying a brown mop bucket.

Soon they got to the exact place where they'd found the red-legged frog, and they slid down to the water's edge.

Edward looked into the bucket through the screen. "Charley," he said softly, "look. He's getting ready to jump. He's smiling!"

Charley slipped the screen off the top of the bucket and gently cupped the frog in his hands. He carefully set him down at the edge of the lake.

The red-legged frog sat very still. The boys were still, too, watching him. Then suddenly the frog leaped into the air. He leaped as high and as far as he had when he flew out of the Conroys' back yard. And he landed in the water with a satisfying splash.

Last Choice: Acting

On the first day of his new semester, Jason came home from middle school in a black mood. He slammed the front door so hard that the dishes rattled in the cupboards. And then he stomped down the hallway and slammed the door to his own room just as hard.

Edward and his mother were sitting at the kitchen table, eating some of the chocolate chip cookie dough they had just made. They were trying to decide how much of the dough to make into cookies and how much of it to put into the fridge for later.

Edward was in favor of making most of the

dough into cookies. He'd already preheated the oven and gotten out the baking sheets.

Mrs. Fraser, who preferred eating cookie dough to eating cookies, thought they should bake only half the dough and keep the rest.

"It'll all just get eaten if it's in the fridge," Edward reminded his mother.

"It might," she allowed. "But it might not. This time we might just leave it there and then bake fresh cookies with it when the first batch is gone."

"Mom . . ." said Edward.

"Yes?"

"That's what you said last time. And there wasn't any dough left to bake when the first batch was gone."

"There wasn't?" she asked.

"There wasn't."

"What happened to it?"

"Mo-om!" objected Edward. "You ate it, that's what happened to it."

Mrs. Fraser frowned. "Edward," she said, "that's not fair. I'm not the only one in this family who likes chocolate chip cookie dough."

It was true. Mr. Fraser liked cookie dough better than cookies, too.

"Well then, you and Dad," said Edward.

"And I gave some to Charley," added Mrs. Fraser.

"Then you and Dad and Charley," said Edward.

"And I bet you and Jason had some, too, didn't you?"

Edward hesitated. "Probably," he said.

"There," said Mrs. Fraser. "See?"

Edward was silent. So was his mother.

"See what?" Edward asked finally.

"I'm not sure," his mother answered. "I've lost track."

Mrs. Fraser was wearing her normal clothing. But she had on her clown's makeup. Her face was covered with white. Heavy black lines drawn around her eyes made her look happy and sad at the same time. On each cheek she had a round red circle. And her lips were painted into a mouth that looked ready to give someone a kiss. She had on a gold-colored headband that had a wobbly gold antenna sticking up on one side with a purple paper flower stuck onto its tip. And the red clown nose she wore when she was clowning lay on the table next to the large bowl of cookie dough.

"What was it we were trying to decide?" his

mother asked, distracted now by the sound of Jason's stomping, angry footsteps coming toward the kitchen.

"Nothing," said Edward, taking advantage of her confusion. "We've already decided. This time we're going to bake all the dough into cookies."

He got up, took the bowl over to the counter, and started carefully dropping dough onto the baking sheets. "Next time we can keep some dough in the fridge."

His mother frowned. "Was that what we decided?" she asked.

"About what?" Jason asked grumpily as he came into the kitchen.

"What about what?" asked Edward, not looking up from his task.

"What do you mean, 'what about what'?" hollered his brother, getting red in the face.

Mrs. Fraser stood up and put her hand on Jason's shoulder. "Temper, Jason, temper," she reminded him. "No need to shout."

"Yes there is a need to shout!" Jason shouted.

"Jason!" his mother said. "Sit down and try to get hold of yourself." She pointed to the chair Edward had been sitting in. Jason threw himself angrily down into the chair. He threw himself into it so hard it almost went over backwards. "Whoah-oh!" he cried, grabbing on to the edge of the table, which started to tip over, too.

"Whoah-oh!" cried Mrs. Fraser as she threw herself across the top of the table to steady it.

Jason managed to keep himself from falling over backwards.

Mrs. Fraser managed to keep the table from tipping over sideways.

Edward, who was watching them, did not manage to keep himself from cracking up. He laughed until his stomach started to hurt. And then he lay down on the kitchen floor and laughed some more, kicking his legs up into the air and rolling back and forth.

"Stop, stop!" Edward cried. "I can't stand it!"

Jason and Mrs. Fraser just stared at him. Jason's cheeks were bright red, and so were his ears. Mrs. Fraser had white baking flour, bits of butter, and a few squashed chocolate chips all over the front of her navy blue shirt.

"Stop what?" they both asked.

"Stop making me laugh!" roared Edward. "My stomach hurts."

"I could *make* you stop laughing, if that's what you mean," Jason threatened, getting up and standing over his brother with one fist raised.

"Jason!" warned Mrs. Fraser.

Edward stopped laughing and scrambled to his feet. "That is *not* what I mean," he replied, returning to the cookies.

"Jason, what in the world is wrong?" asked Mrs. Fraser, sitting down again and brushing the flour and smashed chips and bits of butter off her shirt and back onto the tabletop.

"Everything," said Jason darkly.

"Everything?" his mother echoed. "Really? Everything?"

"Okay," said Jason. "Not everything." His mother nodded, appreciating his honesty. "But something really important." She waited, listening. Edward stopped dropping cookie dough onto the baking sheets. He waited, listening.

"Something terrible has happened," Jason said. "And there's nothing I can do about it."

His voice broke. He sounded as if he might cry!

Edward was alarmed. "Jason," he said, "want some cookie dough before I bake it all?"

Jason looked down at the table with his dark, angry, ready-to-cry face. "Yeah," he said.

Edward put a little cookie dough into a measuring cup. He started to take it over to his brother. But when he saw Jason's dark face and his slumping shoulders, he stopped to put in some more.

Then he slipped the cookie dough and a spoon in front of Jason and went back to the counter to get on with his baking.

"Want some milk with that?" Mrs. Fraser asked.

Jason nodded yes.

She got up and poured some milk into his favorite mug, the mug with the picture of the Beatles on the side. Then she sat down again.

Jason didn't eat the cookie dough. He didn't drink the milk. But he didn't cry, either.

"What's happened?" his mother asked. "You'll feel better if you talk about it, Jason. You know that always helps."

Jason looked as if he might not want to feel better.

Finally he said, "I got my new class schedule today."

Mrs. Fraser waited. Edward perked up his ears.

"We only get one elective, you know," he complained.

"I remember," his mother told him. "Until next year."

"This is *this* year," he reminded her.

"Yes, I know," she said.

"We only get one elective—*one*! Out of six classes, we only get to choose one class we really want to take. *One*!"

Mrs. Fraser began to understand what Jason was getting at. "And you chose . . . ?"

"And I chose Introduction to Computer Programming."

"And you got . . . ?"

"Acting."

Jason's voice was so low, Edward couldn't hear what he said. "What?" he asked. "What did you get?"

"Aaaactiiiing!" hollered Jason. *"Acting!"*

"Acting?" asked Edward. "What's acting?"

"Acting," Mrs. Fraser said. "You know, being an actor. In plays. Or in movies. Or on TV. Or in the circus. Acting."

"Oh! *Acting!* Neat!" said Edward.

Jason took a deep, deep breath. He shook his head. Then he spooned up some cookie dough and drank some milk.

"Did you talk to your adviser?" Mrs. Fraser asked.

"Yep."

"And?"

"And everybody can't get the elective they want. The computer programming class was too crowded."

"Was there any other class you wanted except computer programming?" his mother asked.

"Yep."

Mrs. Fraser waited. Her gold antenna and purple paper flower wobbled.

"My second choice was History of Rock and Roll."

"Class was full?"

"Overflowing." Jason ate some more cookie dough and drank some more milk. "Third choice," he went on more calmly, "Photography."

"Class filled?" said his mother.

"Jam-packed."

"How do they decide who gets into what classes, anyway?" Edward asked, sliding the first baking sheet into the oven and setting the timer.

"By computer," Jason explained. "They feed in your academic classes and your lunch hour and what time you have PE, and then the computer comes up with your schedule. And with your *one measly* elective."

"So it's the computer's fault!" said Edward, trying to be helpful.

"It's Ms. Rushokoff's fault, actually," said Jason, squinching his eyes in anger.

"Ms. Rushokoff?" his mother asked. "Your nice English teacher?"

"Nice!" snorted Jason. "So nice that she

switched me to an honors English class for second semester and it wrecked my schedule. And landed me in Acting. It's all Rushokoff's fault."

"*Ms.* Rushokoff," Mrs. Fraser corrected. Then, "It's good to be in honors English, though, isn't it, Jason?"

"I don't think so," he replied.

"What's honors English?" Edward asked.

"That means Jason is very good at English and that he's ready for a higher-level English class where there'll be more challenging and more interesting work for him to do—" explained Mrs. Fraser.

"You can stop right there," Jason interrupted.

"Stop right where?" asked his mother.

"Right there at *more*," he said. "There will be *more*—more *work*. More *homework*. That's what there will be more of."

"Jason," said Mrs. Fraser, trying to be reassuring but feeling unable to do a very good job of it, sitting there in her clown makeup with her wobbly antenna and her messed-up shirt. She took off the headband and began again. "Jason, honors English will be more challenging and more interesting for you, not just more work. Really. You'll see."

Jason slumped in his chair and stuck his hands into the front pockets of his jeans. He didn't answer.

The three Frasers remained silent.

The only sound in the kitchen was the tick-ticking of the timer.

Soon the very pleasant smell of almost-baked chocolate chip cookies surrounded them.

Slowly, the worry left Mrs. Fraser's eyes.

Slowly, Jason sat up straight at the table and finished drinking his milk.

And as he took the tray of perfect, round, fragrant cookies out of the oven, Edward said, "We put pecans in this time, Jason, instead of walnuts." Edward knew Jason preferred pecans. "And we used milk-chocolate chips instead of bittersweet ones." Edward knew Jason preferred milk chocolate.

"I know," Jason answered quite civilly, "I could tell from the dough."

"Right," said Edward. "I forgot." He set the baking sheet on the counter to cool and slid the other one into the oven. Then he reset the timer. "It might be fun, Jas," he said timidly.

"What might be fun?" asked Jason.

"Acting."

Mrs. Fraser rolled her eyes but didn't say a

word. Jason didn't look at his brother, and he didn't answer him. The timer ticked.

"Well, it might be," said Edward in a small voice.

Mrs. Fraser raised her real eyebrows, which were under her drawn-on, pointy clownish brows, at her son. She was trying to signal him to stop saying things. "You look funny when you do that, Mom," Edward told her, laughing.

"I'm supposed to look funny," she answered. "I'm a clown."

More silence. No sound now in the kitchen except the timer ticking.

"What are you thinking, Jason?" Mrs. Fraser asked kindly.

"I'm thinking about whether to kill Edward now," Jason answered, "or whether I should wait until later."

He pushed back his chair and marched out of the kitchen.

The timer rang.

Edward took the second batch of cookies out of the oven.

"The first ones have cooled off enough to eat," he told his mother. "Want one?"

"Sure," she said.

Using a spatula, Edward took two of the cookies

off the baking sheet and put them onto a plate. He brought the plate over to the table and set it down. Then he sat in what had been Jason's chair, leaned toward his mother, and motioned for her to lean toward him. Their heads almost touched. He glanced toward the kitchen doorway to make sure Jason hadn't come back. Then he whispered, "I think Acting would be fun! I would love to take Acting!"

His mother smiled. "Me too," she whispered back, helping herself to the bigger of the two cookies.

Mrs. Fraser did everything she could think of to try to help Jason adjust to Acting.

She pointed out how rich some movie actors are.

"Hah," he countered. "What about certain computer programmers?"

Then she pointed out how much fun it would be to pretend you were somebody else. It would be like living many different lives instead of just one, she said.

Jason stared at her blankly. "What would be fun about that?" he wanted to know. "I'm having enough trouble living just one life!"

She asked him about his acting teacher, Mr. Warren.

"He thinks he's Shakespeare," Jason replied sarcastically.

She asked him what, exactly, Mr. Warren was planning to teach the class about acting.

"Basic acting skills," Jason said, mimicking Mr. Warren's deep voice and dramatic way of speaking, no matter what he was saying.

"What does that mean you'll be working on, exactly?" asked his mother.

"Voice," mumbled Jason.

"And?"

"Movement," grumbled Jason.

"And?"

"E-nun-ci-a-tion," enunciated Jason.

"And?"

" 'Learning how to cast a spell over an audience,' " Jason mimicked his teacher.

"And?"

"And memorizing thousands of lines for acting in scenes from famous plays," seethed Jason.

"And?"

"And then performing the darn scenes in front of the whole school and the parents and everybody," said Jason, looking sour and desperate all at once.

"Oh," said his mother, "I didn't know you'd actually be performing! Then I'll get to see you act again!"

"Yep, you will," said Jason miserably. "Why does that make you happy?"

"I'm sorry, Jason," his mother apologized. "I forgot for a second how you feel about this. I was just thinking about how much fun it would be for me to see you acting again in a scene from another famous play."

"What do you think would be fun about that?" inquired Jason.

"Well," his mother said, "you were very good last year in *Peter Pan*. You have a pleasing voice. You have a nice way of speaking. You have a strong, graceful, athletic body. And by the end of this class, you might actually start to enjoy acting, and to enjoy yourself, and to enjoy doing your scene, and to enjoy working with the other actors, and to enjoy performing in front of—"

"Stop!" said Jason, holding up both hands in front of him. "Just—stop."

"Sorry," said his mother.

"It's okay," he said, backing away with his hands still held up, as if he were training a dog to stay where it was. "Just—stop."

Later that week, Mrs. Fraser tried to help Jason by telling him about her own acting experiences. She told him about some acting she'd done when she was a kid.

"My parents sent me to Mrs. Epstein's Little Theater Acting School," she told him.

"Why?" he asked, looking up from *A Tale of Two Cities*, a long, hard book that he had to read and write a report about for his honors English class.

"Why?" she echoed.

"Yeah, why? Why did Grandma and Grandpa do that to you?"

"They didn't do it *to* me, Jason. They did it *for* me."

"*For* you, then," Jason said, giving in. He didn't have time for a long talk. Not with honors English assignments hanging over his head. Not with scenes from plays to memorize.

"Well, for one thing, I wanted to go," said his mother. "And for another . . ." She stopped. She wasn't sure why her parents had sent her to Mrs. Epstein's acting school, except that she'd wanted to go.

She'd wanted to be in plays, to wear costumes and makeup, to perform in front of people. The whole idea of the theater, the lights, the scenery, the cast of characters relying on one another to make the performance work, the memorizing and the rehearsing, the gradual coming together of the play, and finally the excitement of the performance, and the thrill of hearing the applause at the end. She had wanted all of it.

"For another thing?" prompted Jason.

"That was the only reason," his mother admitted. "I wanted to go."

"Then it was nice of them to send you," he said.

"Yes, it was."

"And I have to get back to my homework."

"Okay."

Mrs. Fraser wandered off. She was thinking of one play she'd been in at Mrs. Epstein's where she'd spent the whole time disguised as an old woman, sitting on a bench, with her hands resting on a cane, all covered with a black cloak and a large black hood, pretending to sleep. And then at the end—at the very end—she had jumped up off the bench, thrown away her cloak and cane, and revealed her true self: a princess, wearing a sparkling crown and a pink satin dress.

Everyone else in the cast had pretended to be amazed, and then they'd cheered with joy. She couldn't remember why they were supposed to be so happy. And the audience had gasped in surprise. Or at least she thought they had. Anyway, it had been a wonderful moment.

Of course, Mrs. Fraser remembered, she'd had only one line to learn: "I am the princess!" she had cried as she cast away her old woman's disguise. "I am the princess!"

It hadn't been a hard part. But it had been a very satisfying one.

She couldn't think of any way to share any of this long-ago satisfaction with Jason. And she realized she ought to stop trying. It didn't matter a bit to him that she had once appeared onstage as a princess dressed in pink satin. Why would it?

Mrs. Fraser went to practice her juggling. She was behind in juggling. Most people in her Beginning Juggling class were already juggling four balls. One woman was working with five. Mrs. Fraser was still struggling with three. She had her work cut out for her. And Jason had his work cut out for him.

As she tossed the balls—two, then three—up into the air over and over again, sometimes catching them and sometimes not, Mrs. Fraser wondered what scene from what famous play Jason would be in. She hoped he would get to do something from Shakespeare.

Mrs. Fraser had to admit it to herself, she was looking forward to Jason's performance, even if he wasn't.

The Birthday List

Once Edward started thinking about acting and about plays, the theater interested him more than anything else.

He staggered home from the library with piles of books about the theater: *Beginning Acting, Making Scenery, Writing Plays, How to Become a Director, Famous Stage Actors, Plays for Children, What Does a Stage Manager Do?, Where to Find the Props You Need, Costumes Made Easy.*

Soon he'd read every single book in the children's section of the library that had anything to do with the theater. He read them at breakfast, he read them after he finished doing his homework, he read them instead of watching TV or playing video games. He read them with a flashlight underneath his covers at night when he was supposed to be asleep.

Since he was an artist, Edward was interested especially in designing scenery and in drawing costumes. He didn't mind making up plays in his head, but he didn't have any patience at all for writing them down.

"You could do the scenery and the costumes for plays that are already written," his mother suggested. "You know, every time a new production of a play is put on, the scenery and the costumes are different. Why don't you take a play or a story that's already written and make drawings of the way you would want it to look if you were putting on a new production of the play?"

Edward liked that idea. And he had another idea he liked even more. His birthday was coming. Instead of a big party at home, he wanted his mother to take him and a few friends to see a play.

"I've never seen a professional play," he explained. "School plays and reading books about plays are fun. But now I'm ready for the real thing. I want to go to a real theater. I want to see real actors acting in a real play."

When Jason heard this, he made a gagging

sound. But Mr. and Mrs. Fraser thought it was a good idea. They hadn't been to see a play in a long time either, and they thought it would be a wonderful way to celebrate Edward's ninth birthday.

Mrs. Fraser started reading about every play that was being produced in the area. There were a lot of plays around. But most of them weren't plays that would interest children. Most of them were plays for adults.

"Check the musicals," Mr. Fraser suggested. "Musicals make good family entertainment."

But Mrs. Fraser decided that the few musicals that were playing wouldn't do.

Edward began to feel discouraged. "I don't think you'll ever find a play that will be right, Mom," he said. "Why don't you just choose one? I don't even care what it is. I just want to see a play."

But his mother didn't want to give up. "Let's wait a little longer, Edward," she said. "I have a feeling something wonderful will come up. I'll keep watching. I'm keeping my eye on anything that's being produced anyplace, as far as fifty miles in any direction. I'm looking at the professional plays and the college plays and the high school plays and the community theater plays and the plays that are coming from other cities. One of these plays is going to be just right. I know it. I have this feeling. Trust me."

Edward knew better than to argue with any of his mother's "feelings." She trusted her feelings, and she expected the rest of the family to trust them, too. He didn't argue, but he wished she would get on with it.

One dreary Sunday morning, Mrs. Fraser opened the entertainment section of the newspaper. "I have a feeling . . ." she said, turning to the theater page. "I have a feeling . . ."

Mr. Fraser looked up from the News of the Week section. Edward put down the comics and came to peer over his mother's shoulder. Even Jason glanced up from the sports page.

"Yes!" she exclaimed. "Here it is! Here's our play!"

It was a new company, just formed, professional actors who wanted to do real theater for children! They called their company Story Theater, and they used fairy tales and folk tales as the basis for their plays. Their first production was opening the following weekend. It was based on an old fairy tale called "The Bremen Town Musicians."

"One of my favorite stories, when I was a kid," commented Mr. Fraser.

"Yes, one of mine, too," said Mrs. Fraser.

"I've never heard of it," said Jason, going back to sports.

"Me neither," said Edward, sounding a little disappointed.

"Don't worry about that," said Mrs. Fraser. "I'll read the story to you before we go to see the play. It'll be fun to see how the players interpret the story we've read."

"Interpret?" asked Edward.

"How they change it for the stage," his mother replied. "A story is one thing. A play is another. They'll have to make changes so it'll be interesting for people to watch."

"And they'll have to have costumes and lighting and scenery," Edward commented, remembering stuff from the books he'd been reading.

"And they'll have to turn a lot of the story part into dialogue," added Mrs. Fraser.

"Dialogue?" Edward asked.

"Talking," she explained. "What you have to do now, Edward, is decide on a few friends to ask to your theater party and call them up to invite them."

"Not too many, Edward," said Mr. Fraser.

"Right," said Mrs. Fraser. "And since we have to go to the city, not anybody who can't behave."

There was a long silence. All the Frasers were thinking the same thing. Finally, Edward said it: "What about Charley?"

"Charley can't behave," said Jason.

"Sometimes he can," Edward defended him.

"Never!"

"Sometimes!"

"Never!"

"Sometimes!"

"Boys!"

Edward sat down to make a list. He wrote down the names of all his friends. And then he tried to think about which ones would like to see a play, and which ones could sit still long enough to get through one.

At the top of his list was his friend Emily Han. Emily, he knew, would like to see a play. And he was sure she could sit through one. Or ten, for that matter.

But Emily was a girl. Edward knew he couldn't invite a girl to his birthday party.

He crossed Emily's name off his list.

Then he crossed off Jenny Barnes. And Katy Palmer. And Margaret Ellenberg.

All of them were his friends. They all could sit still forever if they had to. And they all would love to see a real play.

But they were girls, so he couldn't invite them.

He looked down the rest of his list. Jeffrey Sanders. Tyler Franklin. David Lander.

Boys. But he couldn't invite any of them, either. Because not one of them could sit still for two minutes.

After he had crossed the names of all of his friends off his birthday party list, he went to talk to his mother.

"I can't invite anyone to my party," he told her sadly.

"No one?"

"Nope."

"Why in the world not?"

"Well," he explained, "the ones who would like to see a play and could sit still while they were watching it are girls."

"And?"

"And I can't invite girls to my birthday party."

"You can't?"

"I can't."

"You did last year," his mother reminded him. "You invited girls and boys, and it seemed to me everyone had a really good time."

"Yeah, we did," Edward said, smiling as he remembered his eight-year-old birthday party.

"But this year is different," he explained.

"Yes? How?"

"This year I'm nine."

Mrs. Fraser couldn't argue with that. It was true.

"Well, what about your boy friends?" she asked.

"I can't invite any of them, either," he said, sighing.

"Why in the world not?" asked his mother.

"Because I don't know if any of them would want to see a play—"

"You could ask them," his mother broke in.

"You interrupted," said Edward.

"Sorry," said his mother.

"And as I was saying," Edward continued, "none of them can sit still."

"Not one of your friends who are boys can sit still?" asked his mother.

"Not for long," Edward told her. "Not for long enough to sit through a play."

"Are you sure, Edward?" she asked.

Edward thought of his teacher, Ms. Black, asking everyone in the class to sit down and be quiet. He thought about his friends. He thought about Ms. Black asking them again. And again. He thought about Ms. Black finally yelling at them. And then he thought about how soon she had to start all over again.

"I'm sure," said Edward.

"But you can sit still," his mother said.

"Yep," Edward agreed, "I can."

"And are you the only boy in your whole class who can?" she asked.

"Nope," said Edward.

"Well then," said Mrs. Fraser.

"Well then, what?" asked Edward.

"Well then, invite some of the boys who can sit still to come to the play for your birthday."

"But they're not really my friends," Edward said.

"You don't like a single one of the boys in your class who can sit still?" his mother asked.

"I do like them," Edward said. "But they aren't special friends. Unless I invite every single boy in the class, I would feel funny inviting someone who isn't really a special friend to my party."

"Well, you can't invite every boy in your class to go to the theater," his mother said. "That would be way too expensive. And way too many boys for me to try to keep track of."

"I know," said Edward. "So there's nobody I can invite to my birthday party this year."

Mrs. Fraser thought. "You could invite some of your older friends," she suggested. "They can all sit still, I bet."

"Which ones?" Edward asked.

"You could invite the Conroys!" she said brightly.

"The Conroys! To my birthday party! Mo-om!"

"Well, okay. Not the Conroys, then. How about Andrew? How about Elaine? They're your friends. And they can sit still. And they would probably love to see a play."

Edward said he'd think about it.

He sat down to make a new birthday list. Elaine Abrams, he wrote. Andrew Kelly. He wrote down Rudy Murata and Alexander Friedman. Then he crossed off Rudy and Alexander. They were older. And they were boys. But they couldn't sit still for very long, either.

He could ask Elaine and Andrew to his birthday party. A pretty small party. There must be someone else.

Edward hit his forehead with his fist, to help him think. He walked around in a circle while he did it, to help him think even better.

Jason came into the family room. He saw Edward thinking. "What are you thinking about?" he asked.

"You interrupted!" said Edward.

"Sorry," said Jason, in a voice that made it clear he wasn't.

"I'm trying to think about who I can invite to my birthday party."

"Duh," said Jason. "Invite your friends."

"Duh, yourself," said Edward. "I can't invite my friends."

"How come?"

"Some of my friends are girls," Edward explained. Jason nodded. He understood why Edward couldn't invite girls to his ninth birthday party. What he didn't understand was *why* some of Edward's friends were girls. But he decided to ask about that some other time.

"So invite your friends who aren't girls," he said.

"My friends who aren't girls could never sit still long enough to sit through a play."

"Not one of them?"

"Nope."

"Not one single boy in your class can sit still?"

"Jason," Edward cried, "you were in the third grade. How many of your friends in the third grade could sit still long enough to sit through a real play?"

Jason thought. And thought. "Andrew Kelly could," he answered finally.

"Andrew is on my new list," said Edward, waving the paper at Jason. "And he wasn't in your third-grade class. He was in the fourth grade when you were in third, remember?"

Jason remembered. "Well then, how about Elaine Abrams?" he asked.

"She wasn't in your class, either," said Edward. "She's in Andrew's class. And she's a girl."

Jason was annoyed. "I'm just trying to help, Edward!" he said, raising his voice.

"Thanks a lot," Edward said, raising his voice back.

Jason left. He had more important things to do than to argue with Edward about his stupid birthday party. He had more important things to think about than why his brother had so many friends who were girls or why he had so many friends who were boys who couldn't sit still.

Edward wasn't happy. He liked Elaine and Andrew a lot. But he felt funny inviting middle-school kids to his birthday party.

He went back to walking in a circle and hitting his forehead with his fist. Think, Edward, think, he told himself.

151

The front doorbell rang and rang and rang. Someone was ringing it over and over again, impatiently, without giving anyone a chance to come and open it. That's either the UPS man or Charley, Edward thought to himself as he went to answer the door. And it's Sunday, he thought, so it's got to be Charley.

It was.

"Whatcha doing, Edward?" Charley asked, pushing past Edward to come in, without being asked.

Edward sighed, closed the door, and followed Charley to the family room. "I'm thinking," he replied.

Charley dragged the big box of Legos out of the toy closet and sat down on the floor to build something.

"What about?" he asked, rummaging through the box to find the pieces he needed to make what he had in mind.

"I'm thinking about my birthday party," Edward replied.

"What about it?" Charley asked.

"About who to invite to it," Edward answered.

"When is it going to be?" asked Charley.

"In two Saturdays."

"What time?" asked Charley.

"It's going to be for the whole afternoon. Mom

and Dad are going to take us into the city on the train to see a real professional play."

"I can come," said Charley.

Edward stopped walking. "No, you can't!" he exclaimed.

"I can," said Charley, not looking up from the space shuttle he had started to build. "I'm sure I can. If my mom has something else she wants me to do, I'll just tell her it's your birthday. And I know she'll let me come. You can't miss your best friend's birthday." He grinned at Edward. Two of his front teeth were out. When he smiled, he looked goofy.

Edward tried not to think about teeth, though it was hard when someone was smiling at you and their teeth were missing. It was hard not to notice how silly it made them look. And then it was hard not to remember how your own teeth had come out, and how that had been scary and exciting at the same time, and how the pictures in the family album of you without any teeth showed that you had looked pretty goofy, too.

It was hard for Edward to get back to thinking about his party, and his problems, when his mind was more interested in thinking about teeth. How they would just fall right out without any prob-lem, if you could control yourself and wait long enough. And how they would hurt and bleed if you got impatient and pulled them out too soon. And how your tongue would not leave a tooth alone, once it got loose, but had to play with it and nudge it and fiddle with it all the time. And then how interested your tongue would get in the empty space, after the tooth was out, and in the sharp little points of the new tooth coming into the space.

"Stop!" Edward cried.

"Stop what?" Charley asked, looking up from his Legos.

"I wasn't talking to you," Edward told him.

"Who were you talking to, then?" he asked.

"I was talking to myself, that's who," said Edward.

Charley giggled. "You silly," he said.

Edward slumped down on the couch. He tried to think some more. It was very quiet in the family room. Many minutes went by. After a while, Edward stopped trying to think. Instead, he watched Charley build his space shuttle. Charley was very interested in what he was doing. He was sitting still. He was being quiet.

Edward decided to see how long Charley would sit and be quiet. He looked at his watch. Then he waited. And he waited. And he waited.

Fifteen minutes went by. Charley was still working.

Edward was amazed. He started another list. Charley O'Hara, he wrote at the top of the list. Elaine. Andrew. Mom. Dad.

Not your usual birthday list, Edward had to admit. But this wasn't going to be a usual birthday party. And at least he'd settled it.

He left Charley working on his Lego model. "I'll be right back," he told him. Charley didn't even look up.

Edward found his mother in the kitchen trying to glue back together a small vase, which lay in two pieces on the counter.

"What happened?" asked Edward.

"Broke it juggling," answered his mother. Carefully, she spread glue on the broken pieces. Then, very carefully, she fitted them together.

"My fingers are all gluey, Edward," she said. "Hold these pieces together for me. And be careful to keep them lined up exactly."

Edward put his hands around the vase, a blue one that he liked and was sorry to see broken. "How much pressure?" he asked his mother.

"Just enough," she answered.

"What do you mean, 'just enough'?" he asked.

His mother was scrubbing the glue off her hands. The water was running. "What?" she said.

"Never mind," answered Edward. He pushed the broken sides of the vase together until he could feel them meet and until it felt like they were comfortably back together again. Then he put enough pressure on them to keep them feeling just that way.

"Some of the glue is bubbling out," he told his mother.

"Not a problem," she said. "I can get some goop-off at the art supply store that will take the extra off, after the glue has set."

The art supply store was one of Edward's favorite places. "Can I come?"

"Come where? I'm not going anywhere. I have to practice juggling. Lots of people in my class are already doing unicycles and stilts!"

"Come to the art supply store with you, when you go," Edward explained, watching the two sides of the vase and trying to keep the pressure steady.

Mrs. Fraser knew how much Edward liked the art supply store, with its big, light rooms and interesting painty smells, its different kinds of paper and pencils and paints, its artists' boxes with a million small drawers in them. "Of course you can," she said. "I'll wait to go until sometime when you're not in school."

Edward stood very still and held the vase for what seemed to be a long time. Finally, his mother finished scrubbing her hands and came over to examine it. "Looks good," she said. "Looks like you put exactly the right amount of pressure on that break, Edward," she said. "Maybe you'll be an orthopedist when you grow up."

"What's an orthopedist?" asked Edward.

"It's a doctor who fixes broken bones," she replied.

Edward did not want to be a doctor when he grew up. "You know I don't want to be a doctor," he reminded his mother. "I want to be an artist."

"You could be both," she said.

"Not really, Mom. And anyway, doctors are mostly women."

His mother smiled. "It does seem that way sometimes nowadays, doesn't it?" she said.

Edward wondered what she was smiling about.

Then he saw his birthday party list on the counter where he'd set it down when he came into the kitchen.

"Finished my list," he said.

"Who's on it?"

"Elaine," he answered. His mother nodded. "Andrew." She nodded again. "You and Dad." Another nod. "And Charley." Mrs. Fraser started to nod again. Then she caught herself.

"Charley?"

Edward waited.

"Charley?" she asked again.

"Charley," he said.

"Now, Edward . . ." his mother began.

"Mom," he said, "Charley's feelings would really be hurt if I didn't invite him. I'm his best friend. And he already said he was coming."

"You've already asked him?"

"Well, I didn't exactly ask him."

"You didn't ask him?"

"Not exactly."

"What did you do, then?"

"Well, I, um—I told him I was making a list of people to invite to my birthday party, and he—well, he said he could come. But I might have decided to invite him, Mom. I probably would have."

Mrs. Fraser looked very doubtful.

"Really, Mom, I would have. I just hadn't thought of it yet."

"Edward," Mrs. Fraser said in her most reasonable

voice. "I like Charley. You know that, don't you?"

Edward nodded.

"And I'm sure that Charley will grow up to be a fine person. You know that, don't you?"

Edward nodded.

"But right now Charley is a . . ." Mrs. Fraser searched for just the right word.

"Charley is a pain in the patootie," said Mr. Fraser, coming into the kitchen in time to finish her sentence for her.

Mrs. Fraser smiled at her husband. "Thanks," she said. Then she turned back to Edward. "As your dad says," she told him, "Charley is a pain in the patootie. And he surely isn't someone who could sit still through a play."

"Well, he's been sitting still for nearly a half hour down in the family room, playing with Legos," said Edward.

"Unusual," said Mrs. Fraser.

"That's true," Edward admitted. "But he's doing it. So we know he can."

"The play will be on for a lot longer than half an hour," said Mr. Fraser, peering from shelf to shelf inside the refrigerator. "No cookie dough?" he inquired.

"Not this time," his wife told him. "This time we decided to bake all the dough."

"I guess I'll have a cookie, then," he decided.

"They're all gone," Mrs. Fraser told him.

"All gone?" asked Mr. Fraser, as if he hoped he would get a different answer.

"All gone," his wife told him again. "Sorry."

Mr. Fraser looked disappointed. He helped himself to a stalk of celery and munched loudly on it as he left the room. The munch seemed to say, *Don't worry about saving any cookies for me. I'll just have a piece of celery instead. Who would want a delicious home-baked chocolate chip cookie if he could have a piece of celery?*

"Next time we have to save some cookies for Dad," said Edward.

His mother agreed, looking guilty. Edward remembered that the last time he helped himself to a cookie, there had been quite a few left in the cookie jar. From the look on his mother's face, he could tell what had happened to the rest of them.

"Jason had some, too," objected Mrs. Fraser. "So. Let's get back to your birthday list."

"That's the list, Mom," Edward said. "Andrew, Elaine, Charley, you and Dad, and me."

"What about Jason?" his mother asked.

"Jason?" cried Edward. "Jason hates acting. Jason hates plays. Jason hates *me*. Why would I ask Jason?"

"Because Jason is your brother, and you have to invite him to your birthday party," Mrs. Fraser told him, using her no-nonsense-I-won't-listen-to-any-arguments voice.

So Edward wrote down Jason's name on the list and invited him to come to the birthday party, too.

To his surprise, Jason said he'd come. "For laughs," Jason said.

Edward shrugged. He wasn't going to let a sixth-grader with a bad attitude ruin his birthday party. "Fine," he said. "Whatever."

As it turned out, neither Elaine nor Andrew could come to Edward's party. They both had other things to do that they couldn't get out of.

"Small party," observed Jason.

Edward shrugged. He didn't care. He'd had plenty of big parties with a lot of guests and presents and games and ice cream and cake and all the usual stuff. He'd gone to roller-skating parties and kite-flying parties and cookout parties and sleepover parties and parties where everyone went to the zoo.

But he'd never seen a real play in a real theater before. And that was what he was excited about this year.

Edward's Party

Two weeks later, on the Friday night before the play, the Frasers sat down to read "The Bremen Town Musicians," the tale that the Story Theater would be performing the next day.

Mrs. Fraser had found several versions of the story at the library. But in the end, she chose to read the one she had at home in her own *Grimm's Fairy Tales* book.

Right after dinner, Charley came across the lawn between the two houses. He was wearing his pajamas and his bathrobe, his red cowboy boots, and his rain slicker with the hood up, since it had begun to drizzle. He carried a large flashlight, and his mother watched him from the porch until he arrived at the Frasers' and they let him in.

Then they all gathered in the family room and sat around a giant bowl of freshly made salted and buttered popcorn, and settled down to read and listen.

Mrs. Fraser read, because she was the one who most enjoyed reading aloud, and the rest of them listened to the story of the four Bremen town musicians: the elderly donkey whose owners had turned him out to die; the decrepit old dog who had been left alone; the mangy, toothless orange cat whose master had abandoned her; and the rooster who had outlived his usefulness and had run away from his master when he heard he was about to be put into the cooking pot and made into a stew.

She read about how the four old, homeless animals joined together to make their way in the world and to help one another, how they came upon the house that turned out to be a robbers' hideout, and how, working together as a most unusual team, they managed to drive away the robbers, keep their loot, and make the deserted house their new home, where they lived together in comfort and harmony for the rest of their days.

Mrs. Fraser read quietly, but with feeling. They all enjoyed hearing the story, and at the end, they were all—even Jason—looking forward to seeing the play.

After Mrs. Fraser finished reading, Charley started acting goofy and ran around the chairs and tables, the sofa and the TV, the ottoman and the La-Z-Boy, and he made all the music that the musicians of Bremen made. He brayed like the donkey. He howled like the dog. He screeched like the cat. He crowed at the top of his lungs, like the rooster.

"We ought to tape that and put it together," said Edward. "Then we could have sound effects for the story."

"We don't need to tape for sound effects," said Mrs. Fraser. "We could each just take a part and make the 'music.' "

Silence.

"There are only four parts," Jason pointed out.

Charley stopped running. "That's a great idea!" he exclaimed. "Let's do it! Please? Let's do it! Please? Let's—"

"Okay! We'll do it!" said Mrs. Fraser, laughing.

"We will?" Jason asked.

"We will?" Mr. Fraser asked.

"Sure we will," said Mrs. Fraser. "Why not? It'll warm us up for the real thing, when the actors do it. Come on now, everyone. I'll be the donkey."

"I'll be the cat!" cried Charley.

"I'll be the dog!" Edward joined in.

"I guess I'll be the rooster," said Mr. Fraser.

"I'll be downstairs," said Jason.

"Don't you want to listen, Jason?" Charley asked.

"I'm sure I'll be able to hear from anyplace in the house," answered Jason as he left the family room. "From anyplace in the neighborhood," he called back as he walked to his room, shaking his head.

"Jason," his mother called after him, "you can have my part if you want it. Or we can take turns."

Jason didn't answer. Mrs. Fraser looked sorry. "I wish there were five parts," she said.

"Don't worry about it, Mom," Edward said. "Jason doesn't want to do it."

"He doesn't?" she asked.

Edward paused. Sometimes he wondered about his mother. "Trust me, Mom," he said.

"He doesn't even want to listen," Charley put in.

Mr. Fraser looked as if he might not want to do

it either. He looked as if he might not even want to listen. He looked as if he might want to be on his way to his own room, like Jason.

"Well, I hope you're right, Edward," Mrs. Fraser said. "Okay, let's go. First everybody practice alone, and then we'll do it all together. Good and loud, now. Charley? You're the cat—and you're scared and mad!"

Charley stood still, and at the top of his lungs he screeched and screeched. He sounded just like a frightened, angry cat.

"That was great, Charley!" said Mrs. Fraser.

Charley threw back his head and screeched some more.

"Great!" Mrs. Fraser yelled. "*Great*! Now *stop*!"

Charley stopped. The room seemed very quiet. "Edward?" she said. Edward barked and howled and yowled as loud as he could.

"Sounds like your old Tuffles imitation!" cried Mrs. Fraser happily. "Now you, honey," she said to her husband.

"Cock-a-doodle-doo," Mr. Fraser said, in his normal voice.

"Louder," his wife instructed. "Faster."

"Cock-a-doodle-doo," he said again.

"Oh, come on, Dad," said Edward. "Do it right."

"Do it like this, Mr. Fraser," said Charley. "COCKADOODLEDOOOOOOO!!!"

"Yeah, like that, Dad," said Edward.

Mrs. Fraser said, "Why don't you try one more time?"

"Cockadoodledoocockadoodledoocockadoodledooooo," said Mr. Fraser.

Mrs. Fraser thought. "Better," she said. "That was much better."

Then Mrs. Fraser did her donkey. Her voice was loud and harsh: "HEE-HAW," she brayed. "HEE-HAW!"

Charley tried it. "Hee-haw, hee-haw, hee-haw!" He jumped up and down, excited, as if he were on a trampoline. "Hee-haw, hee-haw, hee-haw!"

"Okay," Mrs. Fraser said. "Now all together: a-one, a-two, a-three!"

And the four of them made the same music the musicians of Bremen had made. They made the same music the musicians of Bremen in the play would make the next day. And the music they made was loud enough and strange enough to chase off any robbers, real or imaginary.

Edward was glad he'd asked Charley to come with them. And the rest of the Frasers didn't seem to mind.

Still, Mrs. Fraser wanted to be on the safe side. In the morning, she planned to go to the One-Stop Party Shop and get a helium balloon for Charley to wear tied to his wrist, just in case. It was the only way she could think of to keep track of him on the crowded downtown streets, not to mention in a theater full of people.

"How will I get him to wear it?" she wondered aloud.

"Just tell him he can't come if he doesn't wear it," said Jason. "Make him wear it."

Mrs. Fraser hated to make anyone do anything. "What about if we all wear them? Then he won't feel silly," she suggested.

"But what about the rest of us?" Mr. Fraser objected. "We'll feel pretty darn silly."

Mrs. Fraser knew that was true. "Still," she said, "we'll *all* feel silly. Not just Charley."

Mr. Fraser shook his head no. "No balloon for me," he said.

"Count me out," said Jason.

"Edward?" his mother asked.

Edward sighed. "Get me a red one," he said.

The next morning, Mrs. Fraser came back from the One-Stop with three helium balloons on long strings. She had a red one for Edward, a blue one for Charley, and a green one for herself. While the Frasers were getting ready to go, the three balloons bumped up against the ceiling in the kitchen. They kept their heads together, as if they were talking.

Mr. Fraser had the train schedule in his hand. "Keep moving, everyone. We want to catch an early train. It's a bit of a walk to the theater from the station."

"Why don't we just drive?" Jason wanted to know.

"Edward likes riding the train," his mother reminded him. "It's Edward's party."

"If we don't take the car, the whole thing will take twice as long," Jason complained.

"Mmm," his mother agreed.

"Besides," Jason continued, "I bet Charley's never even been on a train before. What if he gets trainsick? What if he throws up?"

"He doesn't get carsick," Mrs. Fraser pointed out.

"Well, you get carsick, Mom," replied Jason, "and you don't get sick on trains."

"So?" his mother asked.

"So it could be just the opposite with Charley," said Jason. "Charley's an opposite kind of person, in my opinion."

Mrs. Fraser wasn't quite sure what Jason meant by that. "Mmm," she replied.

At eleven o'clock sharp, Mrs. O'Hara and Charley were at the front door. Charley was scrubbed. His spanking-clean shirt was tucked into the front of his spanking-clean pants. He wore a wide belt with a big buckle to hold up the pants. And he wore his new royal blue windbreaker. His eyes were shining.

"Special delivery," said Mrs. O'Hara.

"Thanks," Mrs. Fraser said, letting Charley in. "The play begins at two. I imagine we'll be home by six or seven. We'll probably stop and get some dinner afterward."

Mrs. O'Hara smiled. "That sounds fine," she said. "Have a great day!"

Charley came into the kitchen where Edward was getting a glass of water. He saw the three helium balloons conferring up against the ceiling.

"Helium balloons!" he exclaimed. "I love helium balloons! Can I have one, Edward, can I? Can I? Can I?"

Edward set his glass on the counter. "The blue one is yours," he told Charley.

"It *is*?"

"Yep. It even matches your jacket, see?"

"How come I get a helium balloon?" Charley wanted to know.

"Mom wants you to wear it so she can tell

where you are. She doesn't want you to get lost. The theater is going to be crowded. She wants to know where you are all the time."

"I'm going to be with you all the time, aren't I?" asked Charley. "Aren't we going to be together?"

"Of course we are," Edward assured him. "The balloon is for just in case."

"Just in case . . . ?"

"Just in case we get separated. We'll be able to look around and see the blue balloon up above everyone's heads and know right where you are and come get you. Just in case you wander off or something."

"Well, what about if *you* wander off or something?" Charley wanted to know.

Edward sighed. "I'll be wearing the red one," he said.

"And the green one is for Jason," said Charley, pulling at the strings and making the balloons bounce up and down against the kitchen ceiling.

"Actually, the green one is for Mom," said Edward. "Jason—um—Jason never gets lost."

"What about your dad?" asked Charley, looking up and pulling the strings this way and that, making the balloons hop and jump and bang and bump all around the kitchen.

173

"Dad never gets lost, either," said Edward. "Charley, you better stop doing that. They'll break."

Mrs. Fraser said she'd be in charge of all the balloons until they got into the city. She wrapped the strings around her hand and held them in her lap as Mr. Fraser drove to the train station and parked the car. She held them on shortened strings as they stood on the platform and waited for the train to come. Charley jumped up and down with excitement. Mr. Fraser reminded him not to wander off, and he didn't.

Once they were seated on the mostly empty train, Charley pressed his nose against a window and watched the world whiz by. Then he lay down on a seat and studied the ceiling. Then he ran at top speed up and down the long, narrow car and made train noises.

The few other people who were riding in that car ignored him. Mr. Fraser ignored him. Jason ignored him. Mrs. Fraser looked around as if she wanted to apologize to someone. And Edward watched every move Charley made. Finally, Edward couldn't stand it anymore.

"Charley," he called, in a firm voice.

Charley stopped running and looked at Edward. "Bottom on your seat," said Edward. Charley came and sat down. "Feet on the floor." Charley was too short for his feet to be on the floor. He put the tips of his toes on the floor. Edward decided that was good enough. "Now sit very still"—Charley sat so still he hardly breathed—"or I'll give you what-for!"

Charley frowned at Edward. "That's not funny," he complained.

"I couldn't think of anything funny," Edward told him.

"That's not the way it's supposed to be," Charley complained some more.

"That's the way it is today," Edward told him. "Sit still and be quiet."

Charley's feelings were hurt. He sat up on his knees and looked out the window for the rest of the ride. He looked as if he might be deciding never to talk to Edward again.

Once the Frasers and Charley got to the city, Mrs. Fraser tied the blue and red helium balloons onto Charley's and Edward's wrists. Then Mr. Fraser tied the green one onto Mrs. Fraser's wrist. And off they all went in the direction of the theater.

"Pretty good idea, don't you think?" Mrs.

Fraser asked. "A helium balloon sticking up above the crowd so we can always tell where someone is? I was pretty pleased with myself when I thought of that."

As they got closer to the block where the theater was, more and more families were walking along the streets. And more and more helium balloons were bobbing in the air above their heads. Every family with a small child to keep track of seemed to have attached the child to a helium balloon. A lot of the balloons were blue.

"Oh dear," said Mrs. Fraser.

"Not a completely original idea," said Mr. Fraser, chuckling.

"This is not going to work," observed Edward quietly. "If we get separated from Charley, we could end up spending the whole rest of the day following blue helium balloons that would end up being attached to the wrong kids."

"Well, what will we do, then, if we get separated?" asked Mrs. Fraser, looking worried.

"We'll yell," Charley said. "We'll yell like this: CHAAARLEY! EDWAAAAARD! and then the one who's separated will yell back: OVER HEEEEERE!"

People all around turned to stare.

"Shhhh," said Jason.

"I was just showing you—"

"SHHHH!" said Jason.

Mrs. Fraser was taking stock of the situation. So many helium balloons with children at the other end of them.

"You're right, Charley," she decided. "I really hate to admit this, but my bright idea wasn't so bright. Yelling is going to be the only way. But the point is, let's not get separated in the first place. Okay? Okay, everyone?"

"Okay," everyone agreed.

"We'll stick together like glue," said Edward.

"Hey," said Charley, "that means we can let the balloons go!"

"Let them go?" asked Mr. Fraser. "Why?"

"Because we don't need them," said Mrs. Fraser.

"Because they won't do us any good," said Edward.

"Because everyone else had the same idea Mom did," said Jason.

"Because it's so much fun to watch them go!" said Charley.

Mrs. Fraser smiled at Charley. The rhinestones in her black cat's-eye glasses winked wickedly in the sunlight. "And because it's so much fun to watch them go," she repeated.

Mrs. Fraser, Edward, and Charley helped one another untie the strings of their helium balloons.

"All at once, now," said Mrs. Fraser.

"One, two, three, go!" said Jason.

The three of them let go of their balloons. Up, up, up into the sky they went. They seemed to be racing with one another. First the blue one was ahead, then the red one was, and then the green. Then the blue one shot straight up on its own, and the red one began to drift off in a different direction, and the green one seemed to get caught in a downdraft, and then in an updraft, and it danced up and down and up and down but kept getting farther and farther away anyway.

The Frasers and Charley stood on the sidewalk and watched their helium balloons get smaller and smaller and smaller. They stood smack in the middle of the sidewalk, and people had to walk around them to get by. But none of them noticed. They were too happy watching. Soon the balloons were so far away you couldn't tell what color they were. They were just three black specks against the blue sky. And then, finally, they were gone.

"We'd better hurry," Mr. Fraser said, looking at his watch. "We'll be late for the show."

Under a Spell

The theater was in a ratchety old building. Outside stood a flagpole flying many different-colored silk banners, all waving a welcome. A fancy hand-lettered sign said STORY THEATER.

Girls about Jason's age stood in the doorways taking tickets. They wore makeup and long, full skirts, and beneath the skirts they stood on stilts. Boys about Jason's age, wearing makeup and old-fashioned costumes—and also walking on stilts—stood in the lobby handing out programs.

The inside of the theater was as plain as could be. "Makeshift," Mr. Fraser judged, regarding the ancient folding chairs set in rows on three sides of a simple stage.

179

Rambunctious kids with balloons tied to their wrists ran all over the place, and mothers and fathers, aunts and uncles, grandparents, baby-sitters, all the adults seemed to be having some trouble controlling the excited children they'd brought with them.

Not the Frasers. Charley—his eyes wide—held Edward's hand so tightly Edward wondered if he would ever get the circulation back. He hoped so. It was his left hand. His important hand. The one he drew and ate and wrote with. He was going to ask Charley to let go, but he decided to leave well enough alone. Once they were sitting down, Charley would let go, and he could check for damage.

"No assigned seats," noted Mr. Fraser.

"Follow me!" said Mrs. Fraser. Then she took off, making a beeline through the crowd to the empty seats she'd spotted that she thought would be the best. She held her right arm up in the air, so the rest of her group could see where she was if they got separated. "Mom thinks she's leading a cavalry charge," muttered Jason.

Mr. Fraser, Jason, Edward, and Charley followed Mrs. Fraser as she wove her way, with many excuse-me's and pardon-me's, through the crowd of children and adults to the five seats she'd spotted, halfway back in the center section.

As soon as she reached them, she claimed them by putting her purse on one, her jacket on another, her program on a third, and herself on the other two.

Moments later, the others caught up with her, and they all sat down to wait for the show to begin.

It was hard not to notice how shabby the place was. "Makeshift" was the word for it all right, thought Jason as he looked around. The lighting system, he could tell, was very old-fashioned. From what he could see of the soundboard, it was prehistoric. There was no scenery. And the stage itself was just a four-sided wooden platform, raised about a foot off the ground.

Jason remembered what his teacher had told them about the purpose of plays—to cast a spell over the audience, to give people a reality that made them forget their own reality. His teacher had shown the class slides of famous theaters all around the country. Even the simplest ones had plush seats and fancy computerized light boards. Even the simplest ones had the feel of places that could change your reality while you watched the play. Every single slide they'd seen, in Jason's opinion, showed a place where actors—with the help of lights and sound and scenery and costumes—could cast a spell over an audience.

This place . . . He shook his head. Never.

Finally, after a lot of moving around, much noise and confusion, some crying and some yelling, the eager but restless young audience got itself sorted out and seated. Around a half hour late, the play was about to begin.

Throughout all the waiting, Jason noticed, Charley sat up straight and kept his eyes glued to the empty stage.

Jason shook his head. Poor Charley, Jason thought, he's going to be really disappointed.

Finally, an actor, dressed in black and wearing heavy makeup and a long black-and-gold-striped cape, stepped onto the center of the stage and raised his hand for silence.

He waited.

The restless children slowly settled down.

"Welcome," the actor said in an actorish voice, "welcome to the Story Theater. Today's play is taken from an old, old story written down by the Brothers Grimm. It is called *The Bremen Town Musicians*. We hope you enjoy it. And now"—he swept one arm around very dramatically—"on with the show!"

The house lights (as Jason knew the lights in the

theater where the audience was were called) began to dim. And the lights on and around and above and behind the stage slowly began to brighten.

The audience now sat in near darkness, and in front of them, the stage glowed with light.

Everyone's eyes were fixed on the lighted, empty stage. The whole audience seemed to be holding its breath, waiting.

But before anything took place onstage, before the play actually began, something else happened: a child sitting three rows in front of the Frasers and Charley slipped the string of a white balloon off his wrist. Silently, it floated up and up, until it bumped against the roof. There it stayed.

Then, to their right, the Frasers and Charley saw another child slip the balloon off her wrist. Up, up it went—a green balloon, silently rising until it bumped against the roof. There it stayed.

Then, to the Frasers' and Charley's left, behind them, in front of them, all around them, other children, as if they had planned to do it, slipped the helium balloons off their wrists, and the balloons, all trailing their long strings behind them, rose up until they bumped against the roof. And there they stayed.

Charley watched them rise with eager, shining

eyes. His mouth was slightly open, and his face was full of wonder. It was clear that he thought this was supposed to be the beginning of the show.

Then, out of the shadows at the back of the stage, braying and hee-hawing in the most forlorn way, tottered an ancient donkey.

Charley, who had been distracted by the balloons rising so slowly and majestically up to bump against the ceiling, now turned his attention to the stage.

Making awful sounds, the poor old donkey began to tell his story.

And he told it so movingly that without thinking a thing about what was happening, everyone watching and listening—including Jason—began to come under the spell of the acting. And by the time the second animal, the dog, appeared and met the donkey and told his own sorry tale, whatever was going on onstage seemed much more real to the people in the audience—especially to the children—than anything else. The reality of sports, TV, video games, friends, homework, piano lessons, bedtime, all slipped away. And filling up its place was the reality of the play with all its beguiling fakery: costumes, actors, speeches, special lights, sound effects, story. The Story The-

ater's production of *The Bremen Town Musicians* became reality.

And if you looked around, you could see children looking just like Charley, children with delighted expressions and bright eyes, charmed and intent. Children so absorbed in the play, they hardly seemed to be breathing.

In spite of the makeshift theater, the hard seats, the simple stage, and the old-fashioned lights, *The Bremen Town Musicians* cast its spell.

Charley held Edward's hand through the whole performance, though not tightly. And he never took his eyes off the stage.

Edward glanced at him from time to time. But Charley never glanced back. He was completely engrossed. His expression was deeply sympathetic when the four animals, one by one, told the audience how they had been cast out by their masters to die, simply because they had gotten too old to be useful.

He was very amused, full of giggles, when the animals made their awful sounds at the top of their lungs and decided they could earn themselves a fine living singing as a quartet, as the Musicians of Bremen, a nearby town.

He was delighted when they came upon what appeared to be a deserted house to live in.

He was downcast when it turned out that the house was occupied by robbers!

He was gleeful when the Bremen town musicians stood upon one another's shoulders to create a "monster" and serenaded the robbers so loudly and horribly that the terrified robbers tore out of the house and fled into the night, never to be seen or heard from again.

And he was deeply satisfied when the four animals moved into the cozy house to make their home together and to spend their last years as good companions and friends, living comfortably on the loot the robbers had left behind.

Finally, when it was time to clap, Charley let go of Edward's hand and clapped and clapped and clapped.

The actors took their bows and disappeared. And the stage manager came out to thank the audience and to announce that the actors would be available in just a few minutes in the lobby of the theater to talk to anyone who was interested in talking to them.

"What does he mean?" Charley wanted to know.

"Just what he said," answered Jason. "The actors are going to be in the lobby. You can talk to them if you want to. You can ask them questions about the play or about acting or about why they decided to do this story. Whatever."

Charley frowned.

Mr. and Mrs. Fraser, Jason, and Edward stood up and stretched.

"Not bad," said Mr. Fraser.

"They did a great job," Edward agreed.

"I liked the music," joked Mrs. Fraser.

"I liked it *all*," breathed Charley.

"Charley really got into it," Edward said, shaking out his left hand and examining his fingers, one by one.

"I did, too," Mrs. Fraser said, smiling. "I don't know when I've seen a play I enjoyed this much. I wonder what their next production is going to be?"

"I think I saw a sign that said *Puss in Boots*," said Mr. Fraser.

"That's a good one," Jason said.

"I wonder how many plays Story Theater will be doing all together," said Mrs. Fraser.

"It will depend upon what kind of crowds they draw," Mr. Fraser said. "You know how it is with a theater—no audience, no plays."

"But they did such a great job, Dad," said Edward. "They're going to have a lot of people wanting to come and see their plays."

"Maybe," said Mr. Fraser.

"You can never tell," said Mrs. Fraser.

"Well, anyway, today was really great," Edward said.

"Yeah," said Charley.

"What about you, Jason? Did you enjoy the play?"

Jason shrugged, the way a middle-school person is supposed to shrug. "It was okay, I guess."

Edward didn't say anything. But he had looked at Jason as well as at Charley during the performance. And they had both had the same look on their faces. They had both been spellbound.

"Let's go talk to the actors," suggested Mr. Fraser.

Many of the children who had seen the play were crowded around the four actors, each of whom stood in a separate place in the small lobby. The Frasers could see the donkey, the dog, the cat, and the rooster, half in and half out of their costumes, sweaty and tired-looking, standing talking to the children and grownups who stopped to compliment them and to ask them questions.

All of the actors were surrounded by people.

"Let's just wait a few minutes, until the crowd thins out," suggested Mrs. Fraser.

As they stood waiting, the actor who had played the dog saw them standing there and came over to speak with them.

"Hi, there," said the actor, "how did you like our play?"

The actor's wig was in his hand, and his shiny bald head was bare. His makeup was beginning to run, and the colors were starting to melt together because his face was wet with sweat. His hairy dog suit was pushed back on his shoulders, and you could see that underneath it he was wearing a navy blue T-shirt.

The actor, who only minutes before had been a dog, an old dog trying to make his way in the world and finding three friends and scaring away terrible robbers and becoming one of the four musicians of Bremen, now was just a sweaty bald man talking to the Frasers in a normal human voice.

"We enjoyed the play!" said Mrs. Fraser.

"Thanks," the actor said.

"It's my birthday today. That's why we came," said Edward.

"The Story Theater is a good idea," Mr. Fraser said.

"Thanks," said the actor. "We hope it succeeds."

"I think it will," said Jason. "I think you really did a great job."

"Thanks," the actor said again.

And right then and there, as the Frasers and the actor stood chatting together in a friendly way, Charley surprised everyone: "Hi-*ya!*" he cried, and then he kicked the actor in the shin, just as hard as he could.

The man yelped in pain and hopped on one foot in a circle, holding his hurt leg in both hands.

Angry Charley had kicked with all his might. And Charley, trained in karate, was a super kicker.

"Ow! Ow!" yelled the actor.

Mr. and Mrs. Fraser, Jason, and Edward were stunned. They watched the actor hopping around with his costume falling off his shoulders and his bald head gleaming with perspiration.

Everyone in the theater lobby stopped talking and watched, too. Nobody was sure what had happened.

"Let's go," said Charley. He headed toward the door.

"Wait!" cried Mr. Fraser, starting after him.

"Wait!" cried Edward, starting after his father.

"Wait!" cried Jason, catching up with Edward.

"Oh—oh!" stuttered Mrs. Fraser. "I'm so sorry! I don't know what got into him. He loved the play. He really did. I'm sorry—I—"

The actor stopped hopping around. He glared at Mrs. Fraser. She hurried after the others out onto the sidewalk in front of the theater. It was almost dark.

"I cannot believe Charley did that," Mrs. Fraser said.

"I can," said Jason.

"You can?"

"Yeah. I felt like doing the same thing."

"You didn't!"

"I did."

"Why?"

"Because he spoiled it."

"Who spoiled what?"

"The actor. He spoiled it. For Charley. He let Charley see that he was just a man dressed up in a moldy old dog costume and that the whole thing had been a fake. Charley didn't want to know that. He wanted him to be a dog. He wanted the donkey to be a donkey and the cat to be a cat and the rooster to be a rooster. He didn't want to see who they really were. He wanted them to really be who they were while he was watching the play. That was what was important to Charley."

Mrs. Fraser thought. "And to you?"

Jason shrugged.

"This is terrible," she said. "Wait. Stop walking. You mean the whole thing was ruined for Charley? Isn't there anything we can do?"

"Probably not," said Jason, shrugging again. "That's life. Things get ruined."

"Jason!" his mother scolded.

"Well, they do!" he said angrily. And she understood that Jason really did feel exactly the way Charley did.

But things turned out all right.

They stopped for pizza at an old Italian restaurant where the walls were painted with pictures of famous Italian cities.

The waiters, ancient men with sauce-spattered aprons tied around their waists, moved quickly around the long, narrow tables, where they served not only special Italian treats but also delicious pizzas with thin cornmeal crusts topped with Italian sausages and cheeses.

"It feels just like being in Italy!" said Mrs. Fraser happily.

"Let's pretend we're back in Italy," Mr. Fraser suggested.

"*We've* never been to Italy," Jason reminded them.

"Pretend! Pretend!" advised his father. "That's what today has been about, after all."

"What *has* it been about, anyway?" Edward wanted to know.

"About pretending," his father answered.

"About getting mixed up about what's real and what isn't real," his mother answered.

"Okay." Edward agreed to go along with his parents. He didn't want to ruin his birthday for them. "Sure. Now we're in Italy!" He took a big bite of the delicious pizza.

Others had come crowding into the restaurant. The place was noisy and full of people talking and laughing and eating. And the old, old waiters were tearing around, making sure that everybody got their pizza when it was hot.

But Charley was glum. He chewed his pizza slowly, and Jason could tell he wasn't really tasting it.

"I wish the actors hadn't come out to talk to people," Jason said.

"Me too," said Charley.

"It kind of spoiled things," said Jason.

"Yeah," said Charley.

"It broke the spell," said Jason.

"What's that?"

"You know," said Jason, "the feeling you get when you're completely into a story or a play. The spell it puts on you when you forget it isn't real. If you like a play, you want to stay under the spell. At least for a while. You don't want to have to talk to some sweaty guy in a dog suit."

"Yeah," Charley said. "That's why I kicked him. He spoiled it. He broke the spell. I've been wondering why I felt so mad."

"Well," Jason said, "now you know. Now you can forget about him and just remember the play. Remember when the Bremen town musicians stood up on one another's shoulders and looked like something else?"

"Yeah," said Charley, happily remembering.

"They didn't look like a donkey with a dog on his shoulders and then a dog with a cat on his shoulders and then a cat with a rooster on her shoulders."

Charley shook his head.

"They looked like some kind of monster that nobody ever saw before."

Charley chuckled, remembering.

"And the noise they made . . ." prompted Jason.

"And they called it *music*!" giggled Charley.

"Some music!" said Jason.

"Horrible!" Mrs. Fraser laughed.

"And the robbers . . ." said Jason.

Charley laughed out loud. "They were really, really scared! They never saw anything like *that* monster before. They never heard anything like *that* music before!"

Charley helped himself to another piece of pizza and chewed it, smiling happily to himself.

Jason knew he was thinking about the bad guys being fooled by the four old animals. Jason knew he was chuckling over their terror as they fled, leaving all their loot behind.

Jason felt pleased. He knew Charley was back under the spell of the play. He bit into his own pizza with gusto and, looking around at the pictures of Italy, listening to the tapes of Italian opera coming from speakers all over the restaurant, hearing the ancient waiters calling back and forth to one another in Italian, dramatically, like actors, he began to feel as if he were falling under another spell. He began to feel as if he were in Italy.

Smells and sounds and tastes can cast a spell,

too, Jason thought, if you let them. The theater can catch up with you anywhere.

On the train going home, Charley slept on Mr. Fraser's lap, and Mr. Fraser slept, too. Mrs. Fraser rested with her eyes closed and a half-smile on her lips.

"This is the best birthday I've ever had," Edward said.

"Wait till next year," Jason advised.

"Next year?" said Edward. "What's going to be so great about next year?"

"Double digits," replied Jason.

"Double digits?" asked Edward.

"You'll be ten. You know, one—zero. Two digits instead of one. You'll never be a single digit again."

"That makes being nine even more special," said Edward.

Jason didn't answer.

"Are you glad you saw the play, Jas?" asked Edward.

"Yeah, I am."

Edward smiled. "I knew you'd be," he said. "What part did you like the best?"

"I like two parts best," Jason answered. "I like the part where Charley kicks the actor, and I like the part where I write a report for extra credit about going to see a play. It'll raise my grade."

"Jason!" Edward objected.

"Edward!" Jason mimicked.

Jason was back to being a middle-school kid. But Edward was still Edward. He was happy and sleepy. He was nine.